Familiar Territory

Steve Higgs

Text Copyright © 2020 Steven J Higgs

Publisher: Steve Higgs

The right of Steve Higgs to be identified as author of the Work has been asserted by him in accordance with the Copyright, Designs and Patents Act 1988

All rights reserved.

The book is copyright material and must not be copied, reproduced, transferred, distributed, leased, licensed or publicly performed or used in any way except as specifically permitted in writing by the publishers, as allowed under the terms and conditions under which it was purchased or as strictly permitted by applicable copyright law. Any unauthorised distribution or use of this text may be a direct infringement of the author's and publisher's rights and those responsible may be liable in law accordingly.

'Familiar Territory' is a work of fiction. Names, characters, businesses, organisations, places, events and incidents either are the product of the author's imagination or are used fictitiously. Any resemblance to actual persons, living, dead or undead, events or locations is entirely coincidental.

This book is for Rosalie Belcher whose brilliant concept for a magical weapon armed the ogres with bolas that will claim more than a few lives in this series.

Contents

1. Chapter 1 — 1
2. Chapter 2 — 5
3. Chapter 3 — 8
4. Chapter 4 — 14
5. Chapter 5 — 20
6. Chapter 6 — 25
7. Chapter 7 — 29
8. Chapter 8 — 35
9. Chapter 9 — 38
10. Chapter 10 — 44
11. Chapter 11 — 47
12. Chapter 12 — 53
13. Chapter 13 — 55
14. Chapter 14 — 58
15. Chapter 15 — 63
16. Chapter 16 — 68
17. Chapter 17 — 72
18. Chapter 18 — 74

19.	Chapter 19	81
20.	Chapter 20	83
21.	Chapter 21	89
22.	Chapter 22	94
23.	Chapter 23	99
24.	Chapter 24	108
25.	Chapter 25	114
26.	Chapter 26	118
27.	Chapter 27	121
28.	Chapter 28	126
29.	Chapter 29	131
30.	Chapter 30	135
31.	Chapter 31	142
32.	Chapter 32	144
33.	Chapter 33	148
34.	Chapter 34	150
35.	Chapter 35	156
36.	Chapter 36	160
37.	Chapter 37	164
38.	Chapter 38	173
39.	Chapter 39	183
40.	Chapter 40	187
41.	Epilogue: Beelzebub	189
42.	Author Note:	191
43.	More Books by Steve Higgs	193
	About the Author	194

Chapter 1

January 2012 – The Immortal Realm

My face hit the dirt with enough impact to loosen a tooth. I think it might have broken my cheekbone too, the pain in my face was so intense. My body rolled, limp and lifeless, tumbling a couple of times until the inertia was spent. I was unable to stop any of this from happening. Unable to bring my arm up to protect my head before it hit the floor and now that I had come to rest, I was unable to move a muscle.

Daniel murmured a word right before he pulled me through the portal – Incensus. It rendered me instantly powerless to move my muscles, leaving me as limp as a dead fish. It was something to do with the binding I agreed to when I saved Katja and the others just a week ago – a week that felt like a lifetime. Ancient magic that made me his slave and unable to fight the spell he used to put me in this state.

I managed to fight him in Bremen. I wouldn't claim I had been winning, but I wasn't losing either and I fought with confidence because I knew he couldn't really hurt me. I am immortal.

Otto Schneider, the immortal wizard. That's me. Thirty-four years old, a metre ninety tall with a receding hairline and a wife in a coma. Fat lot of good my magic was. I couldn't save myself, let alone my wife.

'Incantus.'

I heard Daniel speak the word, my body returning to my control the moment his lips ended the last syllable. I was in pain, but my wounds were already healing, and I was too angry to let the injuries keep me from retaliating.

Lying half on my back and half on my side with my left arm trapped beneath me, I had to jerk myself upright, but I followed the motion through to leap into a fighting stance with a conjuring already in my right hand.

'Must I put you under again?' Daniel asked calmly. We came through the portal hours ago and had been going through the cycle of attack, incapacitate, torture, lecture, release, and attack again ever since.

In response I pulled on the moisture in his body, my spell latching onto every molecule of water in every cell. I was going to superheat them until he exploded from within. Daniel wouldn't be the first demon I had done this too. The results the first time, when I did my utmost to kill a demon called Teague, had been spectacular and resulted in my immortality as his blood fused with mine at a cellular level.

To stop me, all Daniel had to do was utter his control word. If he could say it, I would return to the limp fish state where I would remain until the next time he tried to reason with me. Ley line energy was plentiful here, a wide vein of it pulsed in the ground beneath my feet. Using it to power my spell, I poured elemental energy into my master – I spat at the term – and used it to turn the moisture in his body into steam.

I would only need a few seconds; I got faster every time I used my water spells this way, but it wasn't something I could easily practice since the victim exploded every time.

Daniel expected my attack I realised almost as soon as I started. With a grimace the only sign that my spell had any effect, I couldn't prevent him from saying, 'Incensus,' once more.

Yet again I dropped to the ground, all impulses to my muscles switching off as one. I would have screamed my frustration if such a thing were possible. I knew what would come next; Daniel would punish me for standing up to him. I was his slave, his familiar, and he expected obedience.

If I conceded and bent to his will, the pain would stop. I would be allowed to eat and to rest. All I had to do was throw away everything I stood for and surrender. If I did that, he would make me his puppet. I would do his bidding, helping him to kidnap humans from the mortal realm as demon kind prepared to return to Earth and rule it.

I waited for the torture to commence, unable to do anything to stop it even if I wanted to. However, this time, the torture didn't come. Daniel paced around to stand in front of me, his feet stopping half a metre from my face. Then he crouched until his face came into my eyeline.

'I grow weary of this nonsense, Otto. If it were possible to kill you, which I accept now it is not, you would already be long dead. I admire your resilience; you have been losing this fight for many hours. I could continue to inflict terrible pain but what would I gain? The next time I removed the incensus spell, you would simply try to attack me again. To what end? If you were to beat me, you still cannot go anywhere. Humans cannot cross between the realms. You are stuck here until the death curse fails. That might be next week or in a decade's time. You will bend to my will, Otto. How much you suffer, how much Bremen suffers, is for you to decide.' He stood up again, the sound of small stones crunching beneath his shoes as he turned to walk away. 'I'm going to leave you now. It will give you time to think. Night is upon Bremen so I think I will visit there myself. The shilt could do with an outing; they are so much more willing to do my bidding if I let them feed first. I might look in on Katja too. Promising to leave her alone was predicated upon you being my familiar. If something happens to her, it will be your fault, Otto. I always said she showed promise. Perhaps I will take her as a familiar for myself, or renege on our deal as you have already chosen to and hand her to Teague. He pesters me daily for a replacement.'

I thought of the teenage girl I came here to save a week ago and what it had already cost me. I would make the same decisions again if needed, and if my mouth worked, I would try to bargain with him now.

He was already walking away, out of earshot even if I could shout, and I was still under his incensus spell which I could do nothing to shift. The effects of the magic used were absolute. No part of my body worked except those elements required to keep me alive –

my internal organs and my eyes which I think were left working just so the incapacitated familiar could see what was coming.

I don't know how long I stayed liked that. I couldn't close my eyelids, I couldn't move my head to change the view, all I could do was wait. A man could learn patience this way. I was in a wide clearing in a deciduous woodland. Around me were denuded trees and scruffy-looking shrubs, patches of grass growing where the leaf litter hadn't covered the ground completely, and moss thrived on old fallen tree trunks. There was no bird song. It was night, of course, but I didn't expect there to be any when the sun came up either. The only creatures here were magical.

After what felt like many, many hours, the sun began to rise and shortly thereafter my ears detected a noise. It was the sound of someone or something approaching.

Chapter 2

Whatever it was continued to come closer. I couldn't see it but listening to the cadence of the noise for a few seconds told me it was a biped. That didn't mean it was going to be friendly or not be something that might wish to eat me. Chances are it was Daniel returning to see if I had changed my mind and now wished to comply, or perhaps he wanted to regale me with the damage he and his had wrought to my home city of Bremen last night.

I finally caught sight of my visitor when they stepped into my field of vision, and I saw that it was a person. Whoever it was, I didn't think it was Daniel. He was built differently for a start and I could see his chin, which had a covering of stubble much like mine and not the trimmed black beard Daniel favoured.

He wore a long coat that came almost to the ground and formed a hood which went right over his head to shroud most of it in shadow. The only part of his face I could see was the chin and a portion of his lower lip.

He came straight at me, his pace even; not speeding up or slowing down. Not until he got to within a metre of my face at which point then he stopped walking and lowered himself to the ground in one motion.

The man kicked his legs out so he almost mirrored how I was lying but facing me like a reflection, then leaning on his left elbow, he used his right hand to pull his hood back a little and I got a grin from him. He was smiling as if something was funny. Then he spoke.

'This is quite the situation you've got yourself into.'

I couldn't move my mouth to reply but if I could, I'm not sure what I would have said. He had an Irish accent. At least I thought it was Irish. My German ears always struggled to discern it from Scottish, my brain too focused on translating the words in my head so I understood them.

Still smiling, the man twisted his head this way and that to get a good look at me. 'I always found the worst thing was not being able to blink. Your eyes dry out and there isn't a thing you can do about it. That's why I'm here actually. Not your eyes, sorry. I don't mean I am here about them.' He chuckled at his own poor word choice. 'You are the familiar of a demon now. You can get on with it and benefit, like me. Or you can resist, in which case Daniel will just kill you. I overheard my master laughing about it. He doesn't get along very well with Daniel. Or to be more accurate, he would kill him if he could. He can't though, and Daniel has Beelzebub's ear which makes Nathaniel's – that's my master – makes his position more precarious than he would like. Demons with politics. You wouldn't think it, would you?'

I listened because there wasn't a thing I could do to stop the man's words reaching my ears, but I was learning at the same time. I arrived here with the absolute intention of fighting Daniel to the bitter end; now I began to wonder if there might be a different route I could take.

'I probably should have introduced myself,' the man said. 'I'm Sean McGuire.' Then he reached forward to grasp my right hand and formed it so it held his in a handshake. 'Pleased ta' meet ya,' he said as we shook. It was a bizarre experience, but the man was being friendly. He was also being honest. One of my unique skills is to hear the lies that people tell. It came in very handy as a detective and for other things in life and it wasn't something I could switch on and off; it just was. Lies sounded different, so it meant that when Sean said he was pleased to meet me, he meant it.

He looked over his shoulder before levering himself up. Wiping dirt and grit from his hands on his coat, he started to depart, still talking as he went. 'I guess I'll either see you around or I won't depending on whether you decide to play along or not. There's a lot to be gained from being with the Demons. They will rule the Earth again soon. Choose the winning side. That's my advice. It won't cost you anything.' He had to raise his voice for the last few words as he was getting further away. Then he turned his back to me and was gone from sight.

He was right about my eyes. Not blinking for hours is terrible.

The time spent lying on the dirt had given me the opportunity to think and what I thought was that there really wasn't anything to gain from continually fighting Daniel. I clearly couldn't beat him the same way he couldn't kill me. I also had to accept that Sean McGuire was right about the demons coming to Earth soon. I believed that and I believed they had a plan to beat the might of humanity. Even if nations could agree to work together, which I doubted, were their weapons, destructive as they are, powerful enough to bring any harm to beings who can conjure magic?

As I understood it, though immortal now, when the death curse finally failed, the demons' invulnerability would instantly cease. But could man actually hurt them? I could conjure magic that would deflect bullets and explosions and I am in my thirties. The demons have been practicing magic for thousands of years and they wield a stronger form of magic than my elemental conjurings.

It might well be the case that humanity was utterly doomed to become subservient to a race who once ruled over them and would do so again soon if they were not stopped. I was here with them, trapped in their alternate realm, and it provided the opportunity to study them. Maybe I would find a weakness I could exploit. Maybe I could take the fight to them.

I made my decision. When Daniel returned, I would act subservient and do his bidding. My only question was what it might cost me as a human being. I know what Daniel does and how little he values human life. Playing along would make me an accomplice to all manner of despicable tasks and I wasn't sure if I could live with that.

Chapter 3

It was many more hours before Daniel returned. Night fell, and the sound of creatures, supernatural in nature and most likely unfriendly, reached my ears.

Daniel approached by coming toward my face. It meant that I could see it was him from a long way off. He paused a few metres away, but unlike Sean, he did not crouch to make eye contact. 'I am making this your last chance, Otto. If I allow this to continue much longer, your resistance will become an embarrassment to me. If you attack me when I remove the incensus spell. If you refuse to comply with my will or in any way do anything that might damage my reputation, I will offer you up to the demons with a challenge for them to kill you. They have never seen or heard of an immortal human. I believe they will have days, if not weeks of amusement, while trying to end your life. Do you think you will enjoy that? Endlessly being cut into pieces, set on fire, thrown into furnaces or whatever other depraved method of dispatch they might dream up.'

I had to acknowledge that it sounded truly like a fate worse than death.

He murmured, 'Incantus,' eyeing me carefully to see what I would do.

For hours now, left alone to plot and plan, my brain had been kept active by thoughts of bloody revenge. At this point, I had to accept I did not know enough to put any meat on the bones of my plan, and I was a long way from fully forming it into something tangible. It had been born, though. Daniel's belief that leaving me to stew would allow me to come around to his way of thinking was going to blow up in his face. I wasn't Wile. E. Coyote, Daniel was. I was the stick of Acme dynamite he foolishly held.

FAMILIAR TERRITORY

Too long in one position, even if I wanted to spring into action, I couldn't get my muscles to respond. Control of my body was back with me, but I used it to roll onto my back. Pain messages reported from numerous points; joints, muscles, my eyes, which I could finally close. When I felt up to it. I raised a hand - a show of surrender on my part.

I was staring up at the stars when Daniel said, 'Come with me.'

Getting to my feet to find them just a little wobbly, lying still for so long had not done me any good, I saw that Daniel was opening a portal. 'Where are we going?'

'To the mortal realm. There is work to do.'

This was exactly what I had been afraid of, but I had a plan for this too. Feigning meekness and surrender, I let him pull me through the portal, emerging onto a darkened street. Looking over the rooftops of the houses to my front, I gawped in surprise at a skyline few people on the planet would fail to recognise.

We were in New York.

Daniel gave my shoulder a shove, pissing me off as he sought to dominate me. 'Time to learn your new purpose, wizard. If you hadn't killed Edward Blake, we would not have come to this, now would we? All that you wish to fight against – yes, I can feel the desire to attack me radiating off you – was caused by your actions. You seek to prevent that which is inevitable. The death curse will fail, my race will return to Earth, and we will rule. In the meantime, I need to supply more familiars and their quality needs to be higher now that the end of the death curse draws closer.'

'You think I am going to help you kidnap people?' I snapped; my anger fuelled more by my impotence in this situation than by the idea itself.

Daniel rotated his body so he was standing square on to me. 'Yes, Otto. I do. That was our bargain. I gave you passage home and let the girl go free. I have chosen to leave her for now. She remains a bargaining chip, though I may yet review my stance if you continue to defy me.'

Gritting my teeth because I knew there was yet worse ways he could threaten me, I took my rising rage and stuffed it down deep into my core. If I was going to succeed against Daniel, I would need to gain his trust, or at the very least, allay his suspicion.

Beneath our feet, a strong ley line channelled magical energy across the land. I could tap into it to feed my spells, using it to manipulate air and earth, fire and water. As an elemental wizard I was able to create lightning by agitating the air, I can force heat or cold into rock or water or other materials, once turning a stone plaza into a field of lava to defeat an army of shilt. I can manipulate air in order to fly, a skill I have yet to fully master but have already put to good use, and I have a plethora of other skills in my arsenal.

I was a poor match for a demon, though, as they can do all that and more, drawing on the Earth's source energy, the very power that makes the planet spin. Wielding that much power, they are able to produce a weapon called hellfire; orbs of raw death that kill living things on contact. That is not the only use for it; other manipulations using the same energy enable them to heal or to torture. There would be more, too, that I was simply unaware of – my eyes were opened to the world of demons less than two weeks ago – I had much to learn if I planned to find a way to damage them.

'What age is your target tonight?' I asked.

'Our target, Otto,' Daniel coached. 'You are part of this. Soon, you will lead shilt to come here by yourself. I accompany you now because I do not trust you.' He locked eyes with me again, daring me to challenge him, a faint crackling as red sparks arced beneath the material of his black silk shirt told me he was ready to throw hellfire at me if I so much as twitched. When I lowered my gaze first, he spoke again. 'To answer your question, she is twenty-seven. A little older than I would like, but unaware of her ability, I believe.'

'How do you know she possesses it?' I was genuinely curious to hear how he found his victims.

'I have shilt working for me. They scan for anyone with a magical aura and report what they find. Anyone who is consciously tapping a ley line gets bumped up the list, but I believe this woman to be attractive. It's so hard to tell when the shilt report attractiveness because they do not understand what makes a human appealing or not. However, if she is, it always adds value. If she can be taught to perform basic spells, she will be traded.'

'Tell me what you need me to do.' I was playing along, partly through lack of options, but also because I accepted this was the best way to help the person being targeted.

Daniel had me use a water spell to break the door locks. It is a simple manipulation where I pull moisture from the air to coalesce in a place of my choice. I then drop the temperature until it freezes which destroys the lock mechanism by bursting it. Daniel talked while I worked, explaining that with the shilt I would come through the portal and directly into the houses selected. All the nonsense with breaking in was for my benefit, he said. I believed he did it so he had time to make sure I would obey.

The alarm went off the moment I opened the door, a loud wail that preceded shouts of alarm a moment later.

Upstairs the voice of a man yelled, 'Get the kids!'

Kids.

I narrowed my eyes and squinted at the floor, unhappy to be a part of this. I heard a panicked cry from a woman – our target – as she rushed to comfort her babies, but the man was already coming down the stairs, shouting threats to strengthen his own bravado.

Daniel came through the front door after me and walked into the house without a care. The man was no threat to him, but I thought it likely the man had a gun, this was America after all, and he might shoot without concern when finding two figures inside his property.

'This is a cop's house!' the man roared, strengthening my belief that he would attempt to stop us in our dread business.

Daniel sent twin orbs of hellfire into his hands. I should have expected it, Daniel cared very little for human life, especially if it got in his way.

I heard the man hit the bottom of the stairs, he would appear any second and Daniel would kill him an instant later. Breaking a rule I had only just made, I chose to prevent my master's course of action, hip-barging the demon out of the way as the man rounded the corner and came into sight ahead of me.

My hands were already up, ley line energy flowing into me as pushed a wall of air at the target's husband. I needed him down but not hurt. However, my soft as can be approach did me no favours as he tumbled from my blast of air and pulled his trigger anyway.

The round hit me high on my left deltoid, jinking my whole body in that direction as the force of the impact tore at me. Daniel was getting to his feet, looking mad as he readied two more balls of hellfire that were most likely coming my way.

Unperturbed, I used an air manipulation to shut off the oxygen going to the house-owner's lungs and murmured a word, 'Cordus,' to bring up a defensive barrier. A shield of magical energy caught the blasts of hellfire, protecting me from them and giving me the few seconds I needed to render the man unconscious.

My shield cannot take that kind of punishment and stay up, so it failed as it dissipated the second strike which meant the third took me off my feet and five feet across the room where I slammed into a wall. From there I slid to the floor leaving a trail of blood from my left shoulder.

My bullet wound was already healing, my hybrid demon blood working its magic. Upstairs the woman was screaming her husband's name while simultaneously trying to calm her children who wailed in reaction to her panic.

'You are testing my patience, wizard,' growled Daniel, standing above me with a fresh orb of hellfire in his left hand. 'The life of a single human is of no consequence.'

'Not to you perhaps,' I argued. 'But to the children upstairs it will be. You are about to take their mother.' I stood myself back up so I could look him in the eye. '*We* are about to take their mother,' I stated, making a point that I was now on team Daniel. 'If you kill their father, they are left with no one. If she is to be a familiar to a demon in the immortal realm, she will return to the Earth when the death curse breaks and can be reunited with her family. That is a powerful incentive for her to comply.'

From the stern look on his face, Daniel accepted my point but didn't care, and I wondered if he might just kill the unconscious man to piss me off. He held my gaze for a few seconds, his eyes narrowed as barely contained rage swirled inside them. Then the glow from his hand faded as he absorbed the hellfire orb back into his body.

'Enough time wasting,' he snapped as he stalked further into the house, looking for the stairs. I disarmed the unconscious man, taking the handgun lying next to his right hand to deposit it where he might find it later. Daniel was already on the next floor, his voice carrying through the house. 'Come out, come out wherever you are,' he sang, entertaining himself as he terrified his victim and her children.

I added my own voice. 'You will not be hurt if you show yourself. Your husband is not hurt.'

Daniel growled at me. 'Be quiet, slave.'

I wasn't going to let him cow me. 'Please come out and leave your children where they are. They do not need to see this.'

I could hear her doing her best to still the children, telling them mummy would be back just as soon as she spoke with the men and found out what they wanted. They cried for her to stay and I could not prevent what happened next.

Daniel, already angry and impatient, wasted no further time. The woman's voice was coming from ahead of him, his body blocking my route to her. He was two metres closer than I, reaching the children's bedroom as I broke into a sprint to get there first.

It was a hopeless contest I could only lose. The woman screamed, the children screamed, and I burst into the room to find Daniel holding a fistful of the woman's hair in his right hand and opening a portal with his left. He stepped backward as I reached for him, shoving the woman through and grabbing my arm so I, too, would cross between the realms whether I wanted to or not.

Chapter 4

I fell to my knees, striking them painfully on a hard surface as we arrived back in the immortal realm. We had not returned to the point we left from, nor to any point I recognised. Essentially, a mirror image of Earth, the immortal realm looked, felt, and even smelled the same, but the only creatures in it were those transported there when the supreme being's death curse tore them from one reality and trapped them in this one.

Unable to determine my exact geography, we were inside a large building with an industrial appearance. The high ceiling had to be four metres above my head, the walls in each direction at least ten. Beneath me was a smooth concrete floor in a wide-open space. It bore the appearance of a warehouse before it had been filled with goods.

Wherever I was, the woman was here too. Wasting no time on pain, I got to my feet to look for Daniel. Having cruelly yanked her from one reality to another, torn from her children and everything she knew, he discarded her the moment he was safely this side of the portal. She was still screaming, wild eyes unable to grasp what had happened or where she now found herself. Having been woken in the night, she was most fortunate to be covered; a man's t-shirt doubling as her nightdress though it did little more than cover the essentials.

Foolishly, I tried to comfort her. 'Hey, it's alright. It's going to be alright.' I spoke English fairly fluently; like most of my countrymen I had it crammed down my throat at school from a young age.

She saw me as if for the first time and screamed again, her face half a metre from mine as terror overwhelmed her senses.

I considered slapping her face to shock her. The idea getting dismissed no sooner than it surfaced. Instead, I clamped a hand over her mouth and gripped her shoulder with the other.

She stopped screaming, which was good. But as the screaming stopped and sanity made a brief visit. She looked me in the eyes and kneed me between the legs. Immortal? Yes. Immune to bruised testicles? Not so much.

A long string of expletives exploded from her mouth as she shoved me away, both her palms striking my upper chest to thrust me backwards just as the shock of pain hit my gut to double me over. I swear it was worse than all the pain Daniel inflicted during hours of torture.

I fell to the floor, rolling into a foetal position as I made a mental note to remember some bits of me were still vulnerable. My demonstration of weakness did me no favours, the woman sensing that she could do yet more damage and following me down with a flurry of elbows and knees as she continued to scream obscenities.

I tried to fight her off without hurting her, yelling, 'I'm not going to hurt you!' and, 'Let me help you,' but she was beyond reason and quite rightly so given what we had done to her. When she tried to gouge out my eyes, I accepted what I needed to do and switched off the air to her lungs. Just like I had with her husband the cop, a simple manipulation of air stopped her instantly, robbing her of the ability to draw breath and causing instant panic.

Intending only to get the point across, I pushed myself away as she flailed at her throat, calmly saying, 'I will allow you to breathe again in a moment. Please do not attack me again.'

Dropping the spell just as the red in her face went a shade darker and I judged she was only a few seconds from losing consciousness, I was rewarded with the subdued version

I required. As she gasped in heaving lungsful of air, I clambered back to my feet, tried to avoid rubbing my nuts, and spoke in a calm manner.

'My name is Otto Schneider. I am a wizard. The man who grabbed you from your home is not a man but a demon. I am his slave and you are now trapped in an alternate version of Earth from which you cannot escape. I cannot change these things, but I can try to help you while you are here.'

It was all too much for her. Having gone from blind panic and disorientation to frenzied assault, she was now out the other side of those and falling into despair. Huge wracking sobs shook her shoulders, making me feel terrible for my part in her misery. Were it not for my plan to make this all better, I might go on the offensive against Daniel again.

'Where am I?' she asked, her voice a cracked whisper between sobs. She was kneeling on the floor, which must have been cold against her bare skin, and hugging herself for the slim comfort it gave.

Standing above her and a few feet away so she could not so easily launch another assault, I sniffed deeply and exhaled. 'In a place called the immortal realm. Your husband was not hurt, I made sure of that.'

Her head snapped up, rage in her eyes piercing me to the spot when she snarled, 'My hero. You didn't hurt my husband when you broke into my house, terrorised my children, and kidnapped me. Take me home!'

'I cannot do that.'

'Take me home!' she screamed.

I chose to give her a demonstration instead. Drawing in ley line energy to power an air spell, I lifted slowly from the concrete, her jaw hanging open as I flew above her head. I didn't go far, but as I touched down, I then conjured fire into my right hand, controlling it with my left to shoot a jet into open space as if I held an invisible flame thrower. Then to hammer home the point, I manipulated the air behind her to push her forward toward me. The whole time, I kept my eyes locked on hers to be sure she watched.

'These are not tricks. I am a wizard. The world you live in is a lie, and you are trapped here with me for the foreseeable future.'

Her scared voice came out as little more than a croak, 'Why?'

As gently as I could, trying to impart that I was no threat to her, I said, 'Because you possess the same magical ability.' Her eyes widened at my claim. 'That's why the demons want me, and it is why they want you.'

'No. No, you're wrong. I can't do magic. I'm just a mom. I teach kindergarten and bake cookies.' The suggestion that she could do magic was horrifying to her; one reality shift too far. 'Send me home. They got the wrong person.'

Daniel's voice echoed through the room, 'Then you will die here.'

It made her jump and I turned to find him stepping out onto a raised platform at one end of the room. It was no more than a metre above ground level, galvanised steps leading down from it on both sides. He chose the left set, pushing hellfire into each hand as he approached.

The woman, whose name I was yet to ascertain had no idea what he was or what the glowing red orbs represented but she was wise enough to see it as a threat.

'Get behind me,' I urged.

'Is that a demon?'

'Yes.' Her question told me at least some of what I told her had stuck. 'What's your name?' I hissed as she used my body as a shield and peered over my shoulder.

'Ayla. Ayla Pendragon. Am I really trapped here?'

'I'm afraid so. It won't be forever though. Play along, do as I say, and I think I can get us home.'

'Soon?' she begged, the sense of desperation in her voice palpable.

It was too late for me to answer, Daniel was within earshot, his strides bringing him across the room. Ayla had her hands just resting on my back, making contact with the less scary of her kidnappers.

As he got to within two metres, he stopped and let the hellfire reabsorb into his arms. I expected him to address Ayla, but his eyes were on mine. 'Well done, Otto. The initial period is often the toughest for those who are not aware of their abilities. She seems calm. I especially like the way you used your reproductive organs to absorb her blows.'

'Who are you?' Ayla demanded, doing her best to keep the quaver from her voice but failing. 'Why am I here?'

'These are things you already know. I heard the wizard tell you. In Earth parlance you are a witch. Untrained, unaware, but a witch, nonetheless. You will be given a period of training and the opportunity to learn. If you prove yourself worthy, you will become the familiar of a demon and will live and work with them.'

'I will not!' she snapped.

The red orbs of hellfire reappeared, and her fingers dug into my skin with fear. He flung both at a steel column supporting the roof. Each produced a shower of sparks upon impact and the steel glowed for a second. It made her jump again, and when her eyes flicked back to look at Daniel again, he held two more orbs.

'You are an insect in this realm and can be squished just as easily. Know that, Ayla Pendragon, and you may live to see the sun rise.' A door opened behind him and two women came through it. One was older, in her sixties perhaps, the other looked to be barely out of her teens and both looked subservient, their heads bowed as they approached to avoid making eye contact. They were human then, not demon. The younger carried a bundle of clothes. 'This is Rita and Karen,' Daniel introduced them, but didn't bother to say which was which. 'They have been with me for a long time and are some of the only humans in this realm with no magical ability.'

Daniel extinguished the hellfire as the women neared him, stepping around to our left and beckoning to me. Even though I hadn't attempted to move away, Ayla gripped my clothing a little tighter. That she saw me as someone she might trust, or perhaps just as someone she preferred to the terrifying demon was a good thing, I would need her trust and that of others.

'Come, Otto. There are more to collect. The women will tend to Ayla's needs when we are gone. Tomorrow we will assess those we gather tonight. If they can be trained, you will be tasked with doing so. If they cannot, you will assist me with their dispatch.' My eyes shot around as I was unable to keep the repulsion from surfacing. He wore utter confidence on his face. 'You wish to challenge me? You will perform all the tasks Edward Blake mastered and you will do them when I demand. You can profit from this arrangement, or you can suffer.'

Ayla gripped my coat tighter, not wanting me to leave. 'It will be okay,' I told her quietly. 'Do as the women ask, try not to worry about your family and focus on being ready to learn when I return.'

Tears were rolling down her cheeks again, but she bit her lip and let me go. Facing her, I failed to see Daniel's impatience. He gripped my neck from behind and pulled me through a portal. I fell back as the ceiling above me changed to a night sky filled with stars and I landed heavily on my back somewhere new.

Chapter 5

The somewhere new turned out to be Rio de Janeiro, not that I knew it until I was able to quiz the victim, a fifteen-year-old boy, many hours later. We took four more that night to bring the total to six.

'Demand is increasing,' Daniel explained at one point though I had not asked a question to prompt the answer. He didn't expand on those three words, leaving me to guess why it might be so. Each time we set off, he took me to a new place, and each time we returned it was to the same warehouse.

When we returned with the boy from Rio, Ayla was dressed, a simple gown covering her body though it would do little to ward off the cold air. Her presence helped to still our latest captive who fought much like she had until she stepped in. Daniel clearly expected this, his experience at kidnapping humans helpful even as it was alarming.

With the sixth person, this time a man in his fifties from Holland, safely delivered to the warehouse, Daniel announced that he was leaving me.

'I want you to train them, Otto. I believe you will find some are already aware they are different. The boy certainly is, I can see him tapping a ley line now.' Then he raised his voice to get the attention of his victims. 'Today you will practice conjuring elemental magic. Each of you possesses the ability to draw energy from the ley line beneath this building. I suggest you focus all your effort on learning to do so. The weakest or least able among you will be executed when I return.'

As his threat received gasps and cries of fear, he vanished through a portal, leaving me to manage them. In the silence that followed, I could feel the weight of inescapable responsibility crushing me. I was alone with them. Six new slaves waiting to be assigned to a demon or killed, each of them wondering if they would be the one to die today. The two women Daniel introduced, Karen and Rita, were standing to one side, still looking meek and still not saying anything. They were looking at me, until I looked at them, at which point they cast their eyes down as if trained to do so.

I started with them, crossing the room with the captives' eyes tracking my route. 'Ladies, my name is Otto, there is no need to be afraid of me. Whatever you have suffered in the past I will do my best to help you now. How long have you been here, please?' I asked.

The elder of the two, for I still did not know which was which, flicked her head up and then back down just as quickly. When she spoke, it came out as an embarrassed murmur. 'I don't reckon I know, mister.' Her accent was American, but her parlance told me she had been taken quite some time ago.

'Are you Rita or Karen?' I asked.

'Rita,' she murmured, her eyes flicking up and back down again. When she said her name it came out as, 'Reeda.'

To the younger woman, I said, 'That makes you Karen. I am pleased to meet you both. Can you tell me what year it was when you were taken?'

Karen spoke for the first time when she supplied the answer, '1847. What year is it now, please?'

I had to repeat the words in disbelief, but I wasn't the only one who heard them.

'1847!' screeched Ayla. '1847? How are you still alive?'

'Yeah,' said Montrose, an overweight African American man from Albuquerque. 'What is this? Why were we taken from our homes? Who are you?'

'You already know the answer to that question, Montrose,' I replied without looking his way. I felt a need to act quickly. They needed to focus on what they needed to do, not waste their time on questions that would not help them. To Karen I said, 'They give you their blood to sustain you, don't they?'

She nodded, unhappy to reveal the truth.

'You said you could get me home,' wailed Ayla. 'She has been here a hundred and sixty years! I want to see my children.' Then she stumbled to a wall and threw up.

I raised my hands and stepped back to give myself distance. When Montrose tried to follow me, I pulled an air spell into my right hand and used it to gently push him back. 'Enough!' When the echo of my shout dissipated among the steel beams in the roof, I spoke more quietly. 'I am captive here just like you.' I wanted to tell them I believed I could help them to escape and that they would have to work with me and play along. Put up with indignities and be ready would be my advice, but I not only had no actual plan, only a plan to make a plan, but I couldn't tell at this stage what level of loyalty Karen and Rita held toward Daniel. If I revealed my thoughts, would they instantly find their way to his ears?

Unable to risk it, I played the part of Daniel's familiar. 'Daniel will return later today. His promise to kill the one of you who is least able to wield elemental magic was not an empty threat. The best thing I can do for you at this time is teach.'

They all looked terrified. I learned their names quickly, Ayla, Montrose, Robert, the teenager from Rio de Janeiro, Gareth, a young man from Wales. Akinyi, a mother with young children like Ayla but from Nairobi, and Maurice, the eldest of the group came from Holland. I wasted no time on introductions, driving home the point that they might live or die today depending on how hard they worked.

'Who can manipulate air?' I asked, holding my right hand palm up to give a demonstration with a small eddy. Only Robert raised his hand. For me, air was the easiest spell to learn. Unlike moisture or fire, the practitioner did not have to create anything, they needed only to use that which was already there.

FAMILIAR TERRITORY

I had never taught before and had to think about the best way to start. 'The ability to perform elemental magic comes from using magical energy within the ground. Running around the planet are ley lines, magical rivers of this energy from which you must draw to power your spells. You will channel this through your body as you manipulate the air. First I want you to all close your eyes and reach out with your senses to feel the energy beneath you.'

It startled me when they all complied. All six facing me in a half circle as if placed there. Blinking to bring up my second sight, Robert was the only one confidently pulling ley line energy into his body, but the other five were all connected to it, thin tendrils like gossamer coming through the ground to touch their auras. Robert's was more like a thick rope.

'You are all attached to the ley line. Each of you has the ability to draw it in. What you must do now is focus on the air around you. Reach out to it with your minds and know that it is yours to control.'

Robert appeared to be enjoying himself, a smile creeping over his face when he raised his right hand as I had done. Hoping I could build on that, I closed the distance to him. 'Push the air, Robert,' I instructed. 'Create a pulse by pushing the air away from you.' He still had his eyes closed when he tried it, the result telling me it wasn't the first time he had done so.

Ayla's wail distracted me. 'I don't know how to do this, Otto.' Her eyes were open, tears running from them in her distress. Though I wanted to help her, I knew it would be unfair to aid one over the others.

'Close your eyes again,' I ordered. 'Those of you who are struggling, think about a time when something strange or unexplainable happened to you. That was how my magic first manifested. I can see your auras.' Several sets of eyes opened to look at me. 'They are golden and filled with swirling sparkles like dust mites in a sunbeam. That is ley line energy surrounding you. It is how the demons found you in the first place. You all have the ability to do this, but I cannot do it for you.' My words were coming out with the tone of an annoyed schoolmaster. It was deliberate on my part, being soft would not help them at all. 'Again,' I commanded. 'Reach out with your senses to feel the air. Your body will channel the energy automatically. Grasp the air with your mind. Feel that you control it and use your will to push it from you. This is the simplest of spells.'

Rita and Karen stood silently watching off to one side until they saw me look their way and averted their eyes yet again. My six pupils all tried to do as they were asked, Robert outshining them all as his confidence grew.

Hours went by, my students beginning to make progress as each worked out how to use the energy they felt. Pulses of air sent dust on the floor skittering and swirling. Many times, one of them would try to ask me a question about where they were or how they could escape. I shut them down each time so they would focus on what might keep them alive.

There had to be one who was weakest, though. One who among the small group was clearly the least capable and it was Ayla. I knew it, she knew it, and so did everyone else. Several hours in, she was becoming more and more frantic to produce an air spell that would disturb the dusty floor. She ought to be cried out, but the tears on her cheeks now were born of frustration.

'Focus,' I insisted calmly, trying to sound like a kung fu master. 'Forcing it will not work. Do it calmly.'

'It's not working!' she snapped at me, her fear bubbling over. 'I can't do it. I just can't.'

The thought of watching Daniel kill her was too much. I was trying to play the role of his familiar; I knew I had to for now, but I would blow it all if he raised his hand to her.

Chapter 6

Several kilometres away, Daniel was waiting for an audience with Beelzebub. The demons' ruler descended directly from the line of beings who had ruled their race for so long that history could not remember a time when they did not. He was the second son of his father and thus would never be the supreme being himself; that was his elder brother's right and one which Beelzebub chose to challenge openly.

Daniel was an early supporter, rallying to Beelzebub's side when the powerful younger son proposed a new, more prosperous future. Their race had always been benevolent, keeping all things in check, letting humans and other creatures prosper and nurturing them. Beelzebub wanted to rule them. To control them in a way that would make the demons lives better, richer, more fulfilling.

His brother, Godfrey, wanted to abolish the practice of keeping familiars, something his father spoke of but never chose to pursue. Their father was clear that he did not approve of familiars, they were little more than slaves in his opinion, but the practice was so old that he felt it would unbalance their society if he enforced such a sweeping change. Godfrey called for it, Beelzebub rallied against it and the sons became two factions, each with their own supporters.

When his father was murdered, Beelzebub already had the vast majority of their race behind him and a hidden army of other creatures, magical races such as the shilt, to whom he promised whatever they needed in order to bring them to his side. He would defeat his brother in battle even though Godfrey would wear their father's armour and carry their father's sword, and when it was done, they would enter a new era of peace where their race dominated the other creatures of Earth.

Everyone assumed Beelzebub had murdered his father, but he had not. He suspected his brother, who, of course, perpetuated the myth that Beelzebub was guilty. Whoever it was, they hadn't counted on the supreme being levying a death curse that tore them all from the Earth to trap them in a parallel version. The same in every way and travelling through space at the same speed, it contained all the magical races except the humans. Their magic was so weak and sparsely distributed it might as well be considered naught.

That was then, though.

Four thousand years later, when Daniel first returned to the realm of men, he found that humanity had flourished without the rule of the supreme being, their population exploding with nothing to hold it in check. They were also almost universally unaware of the magical ability some of their race possessed. The sparseness of the gene that allowed humans to channel any form of magic had not changed, but with billions of them now infesting the planet at the expense of everything else, there were so many more of them that could channel magic than ever before. His personal theory, one shared by many others, was that the death curse had suppressed their ability to do magic. No one knew quite how the death curse worked, but most believed it targeted all the races with magical ability and banished them to the new realm.

Not the humans though, who then simply forgot. Four thousand years ago they were primitive creatures, superstitious and uneducated. That could no longer be said, but even though there were thousands, perhaps even tens of thousands who possessed the elemental magic gene, very few were aware. People like Otto, who had embraced it, were rare. Of course, it wasn't just elemental magic; there were shifters emerging too. They were not of much use to him as familiars although they had been favoured long ago in the past for their fighting qualities, high-caste demons keeping stables to be used for entertainment as one master would pitch his fighter against another for sport.

Daniel was one of the first demons to find his way back to earth, forcing one of the shilt to teach him the portal conjuring. He sensed opportunity and he wanted status. If the demons were an army, he had been nothing more than a foot soldier, but as he secretly stole humans from Earth, trained them, prepared them, and presented them to the elder demons, he began to rise. Now he was in Beelzebub's inner circle, on the periphery still, but there nevertheless.

'Daniel.' Beelzebub had left his chambers, coming out to speak with him. 'I hear of significant shilt losses in Bremen. Explain.'

Daniel expected this, his response was prepared. 'Edward Blake encountered a wizard there. One with significant power. He underestimated him and paid for it with his life.'

Beelzebub made it clear the news failed to impress him. 'I heard of your familiar's demise, Daniel. That occurred before the recent losses. The wizard you speak of crossed to our realm and attacked Teague in his house. According to Teague, you provided an escape route for the wizard and his allies plus Teague's new familiar. Is any of this not true?'

Daniel would never lie as a matter of principle, but he knew there was no point – Beelzebub would already be certain of his facts. 'It is all accurate, my lord. I offered the wizard passage back to earth in exchange for a binding. He has replaced Edward Blake as my familiar.'

Beelzebub didn't know this, the flicker of surprise reaching his face before he could hide it, however, the course of the conversation did not change. 'The shilt, Daniel. You sent the wizard home after you bound him to yourself and could have done with him as you pleased. Left unmanaged, he attacked Teague again, with you preventing Teague from exacting his revenge and reclaiming his familiar, and then he went on to kill hundreds of shilt.' Daniel started to respond, but Beelzebub cut over the top of him. 'I went there myself.'

Daniel hadn't known this. It told him that his friends inside the circle were not so friendly as he thought. They ought to have tipped him off. It was a day ago now that he sent the shilt army to Bremen to ambush Otto. He knew of their defeat, but no one told him Beelzebub travelled himself.

'My lord, if I might explain?'

'Explain what?' Daniel didn't answer immediately which gave the ruler another opening. 'What is it you wish to explain, Daniel? You should have killed the wizard when first presented with the opportunity. Or bound him as your familiar and then bent him to your will. My choice to honour you in my presence is being questioned, Daniel. That is good for neither one of us.' As Daniel tried to speak, Beelzebub held up a warning finger to silence him. 'Go Daniel. Bring us familiars, stop wasting shilt and embarrass me no further.'

Daniel knew he had been dismissed. There was no option to argue, no opportunity to claim his good intentions or victories despite the occasional minor setback. The demon ruler walked away, leaving Daniel to silently fume. Otto Schneider had cost him more than he would allow from any other human. He couldn't kill Otto Schneider, not yet at least, but that would change when the death curse fell, and they were all mortal once more. At that point, he would end the wizard's life and move on with his day without pausing for thought.

Chapter 7

Karen and Rita brought refreshments in the form of water in jugs and sandwiches made from freshly baked bread. The captives fell upon them. Snagging a fistful of food for myself, and swigging some water, I left the group with the intention of exploring.

I didn't even make it to the edge of the floor to look for a way out before Daniel came in. Coming back through a door behind the raised platform, the same one Karen and Rita used to enter and the same one he used to leave earlier.

He looked unhappy and impatient. 'Show me,' he demanded, his shout echoing off the steelwork again.

'They need more time,' I protested, getting my body between his and theirs. Behind me, I could hear the cries of fear, mostly from Ayla and I feared for what I might do if he did kill her.

'More time?' growled Daniel. I was walking backward as he stalked toward them, trying to keep my body in his way, but he swiped me to the side. 'Line up. All of you. Show me elemental magic now.'

Robert wasted no time in proudly displaying what he could do. A confident air spell sent a ripple across the room. Montrose and the others were quick to follow suit, less confident but still capable in their conjuring. Only Ayla failed to produce anything worthwhile. Her arms shaking as she tried her hardest but failed to manipulate the air. A sob escaped her lips when Daniel nodded.

I drew source energy into my body, sucking up as much as I could so I felt imbued with power.

Daniel span around to face me with hellfire orbs in his hands. 'Defy me now and I will kill them all,' he challenged. Then he waited for me to make a decision. How could I back down? How could I stand by and watch him kill a young mother?

Twitching with indecision, I saw him move but had no time to react as he span back to face the captives, raised his right hand, and sent hellfire zinging across the room.

It flew straight at its target, the victim's face lighting up with surprise in the split second it took to cross the room. It struck Robert high on his chest, blasting him backward five metres where he landed in a crumpled heap and was still.

Ayla screamed, Akinyi too but it wasn't just the women as Maurice and Gareth also wailed their fear. Only Montrose remained silent, too stunned to react.

Turning back to my shocked face, Daniel said, 'He showed no fear. He would be useless as a familiar and too likely to challenge his master.' Ayla had already sunk to the ground; on her knees and sobbing from the conflicting emotions tearing through her. The others were little better, but they tried to comfort her. Daniel exhaled through his nose as he let the remaining ball of hellfire reabsorb into his hand. 'You have a few hours to rest, Otto. You will be returning to the mortal realm tonight.'

'What next for these?' I asked, shoving my rage back down into my belly.

'Is that how you allow your familiar to speak to you, Daniel?' The new voice came from a large barrel-chested demon now standing on the raised platform. I hadn't heard anyone approach and caught no movement until he spoke, but it was clear he had been there long enough to hear me speaking.

'What is it that you want, Nathaniel?' Daniel asked, his voice filled with false sweetness. I connected the name, remembering I heard it yesterday as I noted his familiar, Sean McGuire, standing just a few feet to his rear.

Nathaniel smiled in the way that a shark might smile at a shrimp. 'Sean told me your replacement for Edward was causing you problems. I thought I might amuse myself for a while by watching you struggle.'

'You have wasted your efforts, Nathaniel,' Daniel shot back. 'Otto and I have come to an understanding.'

'Oh? You had to bargain with him? Is that what it has come to for you? When you want something, you have to ask your slave nicely?'

Daniel's face twitched with annoyance. The larger man came here only to aggravate him, and it was working. 'Let me show you something,' offered Daniel. Before I could question what it might be, or raise a shield to defend myself, he thrust hellfire into his arm and shot me with it. It hit me in the face, searing pain burning at my eyes and skin as I tumbled end over end until a steel column stopped me.

I could hear Nathaniel laughing. 'Wasn't that a waste? You had a familiar powerful enough to beat Edward Blake and you just killed him. He might be no match for Sean, but he would still have been a useful weapon.'

My skin healed with a prickling sensation as I levered myself off the floor and drew in a gutful of ley line energy. I might be cowed into obeying for now, but no one gets to blast me in the face without retaliation.

Daniel shouted, 'Incensus,' my body obeying the binding placed upon me as yet again, I slumped to the floor.

A few beats of silence followed before Nathaniel said, 'Explain.'

'He is immortal,' Daniel replied. Then, before the other demon could scoff or argue, he explained about my encounter with Teague and what that had done to me.

When he finished, Nathaniel argued, 'This is a trick, Daniel. You want me to believe you have a familiar who cannot be killed. To what devious end, I can only imagine.'

Now it was Daniel's turn to laugh. 'Please, Nathaniel. Be my guest. If you think you have the juice to kill him, go ahead and take your best shot.'

I would have sworn if I could speak and I certainly would have tensed my body. I could do neither thing though, nor even watch to see the next flash of fizzing hellfire coming. It hit my back, searing through me with indescribable pain. I knew what would come next, so it was no surprise when Daniel murmured the word to release me. I knew he was waiting for me to get up so he could prove his point, but it wasn't as if I could play dead for long. I rolled to get my arms beneath me, but I didn't make it to my feet.

Nathaniel's incredulous face was already steaming my way, two fresh orbs of hellfire crackling in his palms. He couldn't believe I had survived and most likely still thought it was a trick. He was going to hit me again, that much I was certain of, which is why I was able to get my shield up in time to stop him.

As the orbs left his hands, I called, 'Dancer,' and rolled to my side to get my arms out in front of me. The shield caught them both, saving me from further pain, but the intensity of his hellfire was too much for my barrier spell. Knowing it would collapse, I was already saying the next word to bring my shield back up. I have ten silver rings on my fingers, each of them connected to me and imbued with my blood. I have to recharge them after each use, but they save my arse all the time.

That I hadn't died was surprising enough for Nathaniel but opting to fight back caught him completely off guard. His disbelieving face could do nothing but stare when I called upon the moisture in the air around me. With my teeth gritted against the pain I still felt, I came off the floor with a spell forming. Pushing energy into the moisture molecules to agitate them, I created static electricity. The longer I held the spell, the more powerful it would become but I could generate a bolt of lightning in under a second – too little time for him to stop me.

I let it rip, sending it across the space between us, the brightness of it so intense it burned my eyes to look. Closing my eyes for that heartbeat meant I missed Sean diving in front of his master to take the shot. Like a bodyguard throwing his body before a gunman's bullet, Nathaniel's familiar took the hit.

Now it was my turn to stare with disbelief, but not for long as Daniel murmured a word and yet again all my muscles went limp. Unable to control how I landed, I found myself mostly face down with my eyes closed. I could hear, but that was about it.

The demons were arguing. 'I conduct my own business, Nathaniel. Do not question my methods when Beelzebub chooses to accept them. The wizard will be a powerful tool and I no longer need to worry about losing him as I did with Edward.'

'If he cannot be killed, he cannot be controlled.'

'What then? Return him to Earth where he can rally others to fight us? I do not need the threat of death or violence to give me power. There are more subtle ways to ensure he obeys.'

Their words raged but neither demon won. In the end, Nathaniel laughed and withdrew. 'Your devious methods have brought you far, Daniel. I remember when no one had heard your name. They will also be your undoing. Beelzebub is no fool; he sees you for what you are and will break you when your purpose has been served.' I heard him ask Sean if he was recovered and was glad to hear the Irish wizard reply. My lightning bolt would have hurt him; I had seen them kill before, tearing through shilt and making solid strictures explode. Perhaps, like me, he had protective charms in place that discharged the lightning to minimise the damage. If I had the chance, I would apologise to him later.

Their footsteps echoed across the cold concrete floor and were gone, the only other noise in the room the soft whimpering of the captives.

'Incantus.'

With control returned, I righted myself and got to my feet, but I didn't waste my energy trying to attack Daniel even though I dearly wanted to. He stood a few metres away looking bored.

Turning his back on me, he spoke to the unbound familiars. 'You will continue practicing and will be taught new skills; skills that will make you useful servants and enable you to defend your masters as you just witnessed Nathaniel's familiar do. Soon you will be joined by more. Many demons have more than one familiar and your role here need not be as terrible as you imagine.' It was the first time he had offered them anything but threats. 'Many, once they grow accustomed to their new life, find it to be far superior than life in the mortal realm. There is no work stress here, no daily commute and no bills to pay. Your master will give you blood to sustain you. You will never get ill or age until you return to the mortal realm and when that happens, you will be among those few humans who will survive.'

'What about my children?' begged Ayla.

'Forget them,' Daniel advised as if they were an insignificant trifling. Ayla sobbed, her and Akinyi hugging each other for comfort.

I could remain silent no longer. 'She cannot do that.'

Daniel rounded on me when I spoke. 'This is your biggest failing, Otto. You care for them. That nonsense when you saved Ayla's husband. It is all a waste of effort. Humanity will be shaved down to a manageable portion of its current volume when the death curse fails.' He saw the shock register. 'That surprises you? Humans are a plague upon the planet. They will survive as a race, but only a fraction of them. The rest will be exterminated for the good of all creatures. So stop wasting your effort trying to save one individual when they are doomed to die soon anyway.' He turned back to face the new familiars. 'You can suffer, or you can flourish. If it helps, think of this as putting your life on pause. The magic that created this reality and keeps us here is failing. No one knows how soon the death curse will crumble, but it weakens with each passing day. Learn, adjust, obey, and you may survive to return to what remains of the life you once knew.'

His words were cruel even if they were accurate. The familiars all looked as miserable as they possibly could, and I had no comfort to offer them. Not yet, at least.

Chapter 8

'Where the hell is Schneider?' yelled Detective Sergeant Schenk as he slumped at his desk. 'Did he run away?'

His questions were aimed at Heike Dressler, his immediate superior who he was always trying to score points against. She intensely disliked her overweight subordinate, a man who would be a great cop if he could just get past the enormous chip on his shoulder.

She spat her reply. 'Why do you ask such stupid questions, Schenk? We both read the same report. His limp body was dragged through a portal at the docks. The charred remains of Zuzanna Brychta were found inside an exploded diesel tank - I think we can assume he fought her and won.'

Chief Muller, who had remained mostly quiet for the last few minutes, spoke up now. 'We have no means of communicating with him and no way of knowing where he is. Heike, you said you believe it was a character called Daniel who took him?'

She turned to face her boss. 'The description matches but without a picture, I cannot be sure. Either way, if he went through a portal, he has no way of getting home.' As she finished her sentence, she swung her head and eyes in Schenk's direction, daring him to make a comment. His loathing for Otto wasn't something he ever tried to hide but he at least now refrained from making comment every time the subject of the supernatural came up: Even he couldn't deny what was happening in Bremen.

Voss, a member of Special Investigations Bureau on loan to the Bremen police from Berlin, stood up. The action got the attention of the room. As all heads looked his way, he scanned around the room to make sure everyone was listening.

'I have just been given permission by Deputy Commissioner Bliebtreu to drop the subterfuge.'

Chief Muller frowned and squinted at the younger man. 'What subterfuge?'

Voss expected the question. 'There is no such organisation as the Special Investigations Bureau.' Muttered whispers rippled as his audience took that in. He had two officers with him who stood up and walked around the room to join him now, Brubaker on his left side, Lange on his right. 'The SIB is just a cover for an organisation called the Supernatural Investigation Alliance.' Seeing the questioning looks forming on every face, he pressed quickly on. 'The Alliance is a multi-national organisation with branches in most countries. The problem you are seeing here has been happening in other places for decades. It may have been happening for centuries, we just don't know, but it is gathering pace.'

Chief Muller raised a hand as he spoke. 'There is an organisation that knows about things like the shilt and you are doing what about it exactly? I lost three officers last night.' Heike was closest to the chief and could see his muscles bunching, he might not leave his chair, but if he did, it would be with the intent purpose of punching Voss.

Voss hung his head. 'The choices made are ... regrettable.'

'Regrettable?' roared Muller, slamming his hand on the table with a loud thump and shoving his chair back.

Voss wasn't going to be placed on the back foot. 'Yes, regrettable, he snapped his reply. 'I was under orders not to reveal the true nature of our organisation. The population is not ready to accept the truth that there are supernatural creatures visiting our world from an alternate version of Earth. The Alliance is working on weapons to combat them, but we know very little about the threat at this time.'

Muller forced himself to calm a little. 'So why reveal yourself now?'

Voss pursed his lips and exhaled through his nose. 'Deputy Commissioner Bliebtreu is coming here in person. The problem here is now greater than that anywhere else in Germany.'

Heike spoke up. 'Otto spoke about the end of days. He seemed to think we were heading for a biblical cataclysm where the demons, that was what he called them, and angels, would return to Earth to fight for rule over us. Is that what this is? Is that what the Alliance believes?'

Her questions caused unparalleled chatter as everyone in the room started arguing at once. How could it be the end of days? Where is God in all this? Where are the army? What is the government doing to prevent this catastrophe?

Muller let it rage for a minute, then called for quiet, raising his voice so he could be heard. 'Last night the city was invaded by hundreds of those things Otto called shilt. They killed three of my officers and wounded others. We need reinforcements here, is that what Bliebtreu is bringing?'

'Yes, I believe so,' replied Voss on cue.

'Then we need to get some rest, people.' As the chatter started up again, Muller called for silence once more. 'A month ago, I would have laughed at the idea of a supernatural invasion. Since then, I have seen wizards and werewolves, heard stories about demons stealing people through magical gateways, and have personally fought a race of creatures called the shilt who can disguise themselves as men using magic.' He looked around the room at his officers, pausing to make eye contact with most. 'I for one welcome any help we can get, especially if they know more about what is going on than I do.' He pierced Voss with his gaze. 'I need to speak with Bliebtreu now. I want to know how he intends to protect Bremen's citizens. Otherwise I will be approaching the mayor and asking him to evacuate the city.'

Chapter 9

The next week passed in a blur, every day almost a carbon copy of the one before. Daniel took me through a portal to arrive somewhere at night. Most times he would materialise inside a house, sometimes inside the room of the person he wanted to take. Each experience was as awful as the one before, but the warehouse soon began to look like a refugee camp as it filled with his stolen familiars. I even used my own magic to assist him in gathering his targets.

He killed more of them, there was nothing I could do to prevent it and though I knew it would prey on my soul and haunt my dreams, I let it happen. To reach the end goal, there was no choice other than to see this through. I would help no one by folding my hand now.

By the eighth day, we had taken forty-three new familiars though he had killed three for failing to please him or to set an example. People of different ages, races, religions and gender. The ability level ranged from those like Ayla who were unaware they even possessed the ability to do magic, to a young Australian woman called Dayna who was using it daily to make money as a street magician. Daniel was especially pleased with her because she was young and pretty, something the elder demons would like. I found the concept repulsive.

It had been six days since Daniel last used the Incensus spell on me, but it surprised me when he said, 'You have earned yourself a reward, Otto.' He saw my look and added, 'I have other matters that require my attention. Gathering the familiars is a task I can ill-afford to dedicate my own time to. Edward performed that function for many decades. Now I need you to take over. Instead of me opening the portal, you will travel with shilt. If you kill them, which I know you can, and try to escape, I will punish you and I will punish others - your actions will impact the welfare of the familiars you have taken. However, I believe you see the sense in working with me, so I will take you to see your wife.' I jolted with surprise. 'That is what you want, yes?' he asked.

I nodded. My wife, Kerstin, was in hospital in a coma. She had been that way for more than nine months now, her condition Daniel's fault so far as I was concerned though he maintained the story that the injury to her skull was an accident. I came home one day to find him in my kitchen and her lying on the floor. He claimed to have targeted my house on the advice of the shilt. They told him someone inside was drawing on a ley line, but I was out when he came and Kerstin panicked in her fright, slipped and struck her head. She had not woken since. Until he brought me here against my will, I visited her every night. Now I hadn't seen her for a week, and I was overcome with emotion at the thought that I might. It was exactly what he planned, the truth of his claim to Nathaniel ringing true; he did have better ways than threats to make me comply.

Knowing the truth of that, Daniel straightened and opened a portal. The shimmering air just behind where he stood opened to reveal the scene beyond as I touched his hand. It was Bremen. My hometown. I hadn't seen it in a week, the view was of the St. Joseph-Stift hospital from the park across the street. It was night, though I knew not what time, the bustle of people outside the main entrance assured me it had to be within visiting hours which lifted my heart. I almost found myself saying thank you to the demon holding me captive, such was the impact of his gift. It wasn't a gift, though, it was incentive. I was being trained like a dog with positive and negative reinforcement.

Good Otto, have a treat.

Getting to see Kerstin wasn't part of my plan. I expected that to come later, after I successfully negotiated other stages, but now I was here, I felt an ache that went down deep into my bones.

I had to see her.

Beside me, forgotten as I stared at the building to my front, Daniel said, 'I will wait here, Otto. Do not be too long. There is yet work to do this night.'

Without sparing a word or a glance, I hurried on, my feet moving swiftly as I ran to get to her. A clock at the top of an electronic display board outside the hospital let me know it was still early evening, not even eight o'clock.

Her ward was on the third floor, the route there so familiar I probably could find it with my eyes closed. At the nurses' station just inside the doors, I spotted Nurse Christiana Makatsch. Her head was lit up by the reflection from the computer screen she studied. Lighting in the ward was dimmed and soft, the ward always quiet because none of the patients ever made any noise.

She looked up as I came in, recognising me, but surprised to see my face. After months of visiting every day, my visits became sporadic for a week and then ceased suddenly. 'Herr Schneider,' she beamed. 'Are you feeling better?'

Her question gave me pause until I remembered that I last visited when I thought I had a winter cold. It transpired that the feverish symptoms I suffered were caused by the demon magic coursing through my body. My blood was changing, which threw the doctors a curve ball, but it also explained why I had not been seen in a week.

Grasping the excuse, I said, 'Much better, thank you. How is Kerstin?'

Christiana bit her lip. 'I need to call the doctor to come and explain.'

My heart thudded in my chest. There was never more than a slim chance she would wake, which meant I knew I was waiting for the day when her condition deteriorated. Though I refused to ever dwell on it, I could not escape that it might happen. Now it was here.

I guess Christiana saw my expression change because she was instantly on her feet and coming to comfort me. 'No, Otto, it's nothing like that. She's fine. Better than fine maybe.'

Now my heart raced. Was she waking up? Could it be true?

'I need to sit you down and I need to get the doctor.' She backed me toward a chair. 'It is hard to explain, and you mustn't get your hopes up, but there has been a change to her condition.'

I was almost bursting now. 'Can I see her?'

The nurse nodded. 'Yes, you go through and be with her. Talk to her. I'll call the doctor.'

I rushed to her room, finding her looking both serene and beautiful as she always did. The nurses did a great job of keeping her hair brushed and tidied. Or maybe it wasn't the nurses but someone else who came around the ward to perform that task. It mattered not. I wanted to hold her and never let go, but instead I took her seemingly lifeless right hand and kissed her cheek as I sat in the chair next to her bed.

Then I cried, sad tears leaking from my eyes as I did nothing to staunch the flow, and I told her about my week. I told her about killing Zuzanna, a traumatised girl who was going to kill and kill unless someone stopped her, and I told her about Ayla and the terrible things I was having to do to for Daniel. The pent-up negative emotions burst from me like a dam breaking, all of them pouring forth until there was nothing left inside me.

I imagined her answers, my lawyer wife giving me sage advice on how to handle each problem and presenting an argument where necessary.

Presently, I heard footsteps approaching and wiped my face. The tears were gone but I most likely had them still trapped in my stubble which was getting long after a week of not trimming it. Nurse Makatsch peered through the window in the door before opening it, then stood to one side to let the doctor in. He was in his sixties and looked a lot like me – hair cut short, a few days of stubble and a lean frame that suggested regular exercise was part of his routine. He wore waistcoat and matching trousers, the jacket to his suit absent. Over the course of her treatment, I had met several doctors, this man was new.

'Good evening,' I greeted him as I rose to shake his hand.

'Good evening, Herr Schneider. My name is Peter Braunsweiger, I am one of the senior clinicians dealing with brain injuries such as your wife's. Christiana made you aware that your wife's condition has changed?'

'Yes. What does that mean for her recovery?'

He nodded at the expected questions and invited me to sit again. He brought a chair from the other side of the room so he could sit close to me and explain. 'In patients with Kerstin's condition, full recovery is rare, as you know.'

'But not impossible,' I interrupted, unable to stop myself.

'That is correct. However, a full recovery would be rare, and I want to be sure that you do not get your hopes up. If she does regain consciousness, only then will we be able to determine the full extent of any damage she may have sustained from the original injury. It may be that her speech is affected, or her motor functions.' I knew all this; the medical team had drilled it into me over again. I let him continue. 'Two days ago, the nurses found that your wife had changed position by herself.'

His words hit me like an electric shock. Kerstin hadn't moved in months. It meant the nurses had to rotate her position in bed to prevent sores from forming and all her blood gathering in one place. 'Did she turn over?'

Nurse Makatsch answered, 'No. She turned her head. She did the same thing again this morning.'

Doctor Braunsweiger said, 'It could indicate an improvement in her condition. We will continue to monitor her and do all we can to stimulate her brain. Your visits are critical. Will you be able to take time off work to spend more time here?'

I didn't know whether to laugh or cry at his question. Thinking I would have to ask my boss, the evil demon bent on ruling the world, I said, 'I'll see what I can do.'

Doctor Braunsweiger did his best to explain what might or might not happen and emphasised that her chances of recovery were still very slim. I took most of it in while I gazed at Kerstin's beautiful face. He left me with her so I continued to tell her about my master plan and about what I was going to do to the demons if I could. An hour slipped by, and seeing the time, I chose to leave. Maybe I could spend another hour with her, maybe Daniel didn't care, but I wouldn't risk him coming into the hospital to look for me. I didn't want him anywhere near my wife.

FAMILIAR TERRITORY

When I got back to the main entrance on the ground floor, I saw three faces I recognised, and I knew I had already stayed too long.

Chapter 10

Heike Dressler might have been at the hospital for any number of reasons, but she had Officer Klaus Nieswand by her side, so it had to be police business. They saw me at the exact same moment I saw them, but it was the third person who made my adrenalin surge.

Daniel was waiting for me inside the hospital.

He had a cup of coffee in his hand from the franchise chain located in the atrium and lounged against the side of the counter as he waited. Heike raised her hand to make sure I knew she wanted to speak to me, but it paused halfway up as she tracked my eyes and saw the demon she recognised.

Heike and Klaus were between me and the doors. Daniel was almost ninety degrees away as I faced them and closer to me than they were. The wide hospital atrium bustled with people - maybe a hundred innocent lives. If Daniel started flinging hellfire, they would not all survive.

Heike was already going for her gun. Klaus too. 'Police! Stop!' she yelled at Daniel as her handbag hit the floor. She was in a two-footed stance, her arms held forward to form a perfect vee and her weight balanced, ready to fire.

Cries of alarm filled the air. There were people between Daniel and the two officers, it was putting Heike and Klaus off, but Daniel had no such concerns. I saw him powering up, arcs of red dancing over his silk shirt. I had no time to choose, no time to devise a plan. He would kill without even noticing.

I snatched at a ley line, conjuring my spells even as it fuelled them. Having no time for finesse, I made a pulse of air that caught all those still between Daniel and the cops; even those with the sense to throw themselves on the floor were tossed across the room to get them clear. Daniel's arms were rising, dirty red orbs forming in each hand to illuminate the grimace his face now formed. He was going to blast both Heike and Klaus if I didn't stop him.

There was no time for me to form a worthwhile bolt of lightning, I might be able to bring forth a flame, but that was too likely to start a fire, and an earth spell would take more time than I had so I went with air again. The easiest and swiftest to conjure, a manipulation of air wouldn't stop this, but it might buy me the time I needed.

I used it to throw a cleaner's trolley. The heavy, four-wheeled, push-along cart hit Heike on her right side with enough force to push her into Klaus and pick them both up. It tumbled as it hit them, Heike pulling her trigger at the same time but the shot going wild. I heard it hit something high above us.

Daniel's twin orbs of hellfire flew through the space she and Klaus had just occupied. Missing the targets, the orbs flew on to hit an ornate art sculpture which exploded into fragments.

The cart spilled its contents, a bucket of water drenching my friends as litter and other detritus covered them. I didn't hang around to look and certainly didn't try to apologise, I ran for Daniel shouting, 'Open a portal!'

He already had two more orbs ready to fling but I was in his way now, blocking his shot with my body. There was no mistaking the anger on his face when the orbs faded and the air behind him began to shimmer.

Heike might not thank me for it, but there was no doubt I had just saved her life. Both she and Klaus would have perished if I had gone for Daniel instead. He would have reeled from whatever I threw at him, rendered me immobile with a word and then killed them at his leisure. Not only that, it would have put me back to square one just when I was starting to get somewhere. Everything I wanted to do revolved around Daniel believing he could afford to take his eyes off me.

Running toward him as if trying to escape the hospital and the chance that Heike might shoot me, I grabbed his hand and ran through the portal to land the other side.

It was not until my feet touched the ground that I realised we were not back in the warehouse.

Chapter 11

The portal only went between realms not across them, so having just left the mortal realm, I was now back among the demons. I also knew where we were, I had been here before. Before me was Daniel's house. Last time I came here by forcing a shilt to bring me across the realms on threat of death, my friend the werewolf holding him by the throat for emphasis. I was entirely uninvited then, breaking in and stealing things I needed to help me find Heike and Katja, who had been taken by Edward Blake and Daniel respectively.

'As my familiar, I need you close.' Daniel didn't tell me anything else, he came through the portal at a walking pace and just kept going. Inside the house, I looked about at vaguely familiar surroundings, remembering how jarring I found it the first time to discover a family home with pictures and mementos.

'You do not have much time, Otto,' Daniel called from somewhere deeper in the house. 'If you wish to eat, please do so. We are going out soon.'

'Going out?' He made it sound like we were off to the movies or something. I expected to be heading back to the mortal realm for another night of kidnapping innocent people.

'Yes,' he replied. 'There are elements of life here you are not yet aware of. This will be instructional for you.'

Typically cryptic, I got nothing further from him except that I would be living with him now. For the last week, all my time when not in the mortal realm kidnapping people, was spent in the warehouse. Blankets became beds when we absolutely had to sleep, and there were (very) basic facilities for getting ourselves cleaned – a set of toilets in the building with sinks and running cold water. Now I was to live in his grand house, a large detached place with multiple bedrooms. Daniel said all familiars lived with their masters.

When we left his house, we joined others in the street who were all heading in the same direction. Some demons had familiars trailing after them, most did not, but all were well-dressed for the occasion; whatever it was.

'What is this?' I asked.

Daniel didn't even look my way when he said, 'An education.'

I didn't have to wait too long to find out where we were going; we left the houses behind us after about two kilometres, entering an industrial estate. It struck me as strange that the demons walked everywhere, but when I quizzed Daniel on the matter he replied, 'Flying is considered vulgar. We can, but we choose not to. It suggests a sense of urgency that in turn implies one is ill-prepared and needs to move quickly.'

I refused to let any of the trivialities frustrate me, following my master, a term I would never grow used to, into a large packing plant. The sign outside bore the logo of a well-known global firm, but it wasn't until we passed inside that I began to get an idea of what we were here for.

The centre of the building had a wide floor; a large open space which had demons crowded all around the periphery. In the centre stood two people, both looking nervous and facing each other as the crowd bayed. Both male and stripped to their waist, they were lean but not muscular. One had very short-cropped dark hair. The other had longer hair and tattoos over his chest and shoulders. Otherwise they were similar in height and build and age, both in the early thirties like me.

They were going to fight each other. I was certain of it. I wanted to ask Daniel why, though I held back rather than give him the pleasure of being cryptic yet again. To my surprise he volunteered the information.

'You may be wondering why I have brought you here, Otto. This, as you have probably worked out, is a little sport for my race. When familiars step out of line, we can just kill them. You have seen how easy it is. However, we gain more by forcing them to fight. It is not always as a punishment though. Because we cannot hurt each other, Beelzebub refuses to tolerate infighting, we can challenge each other through our familiars.'

'Is it to the death?' I enquired.

'Sometimes. That would depend on the owner's thoughts on the matter. Most consider an educated familiar is superior to a new one and there are not enough familiars to go around so few wish to lose the one they have. Death can happen whether planned or not, of course. If the familiars are thought to be going easy on one another, Beelzebub might step in and kill them. They sometimes kill each other by accident too.'

'Will you expect me to fight?'

'Heavens, no,' he chuckled. 'I would love to even a few scores by pitching you against the familiars of several demons, but word would soon get out that you cannot be killed, and they would cry foul. Edward fought many times, of course.'

'Did he ever lose?' I asked, remembering how easily he kicked my butt the first two times.

'Only once. Nathaniel challenged me. I accepted gladly but his familiar proved too strong for Edward.'

'Sean McGuire?' I wanted to confirm in case Nathaniel had more than one. Daniel just nodded his reply, unwilling to speak as the crowd hushed. It was beginning.

The master of ceremony was a demon wearing a top hat of all things. At one end of the rectangular arena, sat Beelzebub on a throne. Nathaniel stood just to his left and there were several other demons around him that I assume to be his inner circle or top dogs.

The MC gave the crowd the names of the two demons whose familiars were to fight, Rameses and Teago, but didn't bother to name the lowly slaves. With a shouted command to, 'Commence!' both familiars, threw spells.

Neither had any form of defensive spell, perhaps they had been stripped of them before the fight, and both went with an air spell. It was a bit like watching a giant game of rock, paper, scissors, as both air spells, a pulse of air intended to knock the other from their feet, cancelled each other out.

They both switched to earth, creating ripples in the ground and when that didn't work, one chose to use a manipulation of air to stop the other breathing. Everyone saw Cropped-hair gag when his lungs stopped working, but he wasn't defeated yet. There was air in his body, so ignoring that he couldn't breathe, he pulled pebbles from a pocket and threw them into the air.

His opponent saw them and immediately dropped his hold on Cropped-hair's lungs. I didn't understand why until the pebbles were caught in mid-air. Cropped-hair used a conjuring on the air to propel them at speed, the small pieces of stone becoming like bullets as they shot across the arena.

Tattoo tried to duck them, conjuring fire as he threw himself backward. Most of the pebbles missed, but one caught his shoulder which exploded a puff of red into the air where it tore through his flesh. He cried out in pain and fell, but his jet of flame had struck home; Cropped hair was burned on his left side and his trousers were on fire.

He ducked and rolled to put out the flames, but that was all the time Tattoo needed to generate the lightning that ended the fight. Arcs of it pounded Cropped-hair and I thought Tattoo might keep going until his opponent was dead. Mercifully, he stopped, his face turned to the master of ceremonies for a verdict while his chest heaved from the effort and adrenalin.

'Rameses is the winner!' the demon in the top hat announced with a roar. He got a cheer from the audience of demons though I didn't see any of the familiars respond. Most of them had their eyes on Cropped-hair to see if he was going to get up. The fight over, Tattoo was kneeling at his defeated opponent's side, checking if the damage was permanent. I watched Sean McGuire, curious about him since he was one of the few familiars I knew by name. He appeared unbothered by Cropped-hair's condition. I told myself there could be a number of reasons for his indifference.

Cropped-hair finally started to rise, but Daniel was already calling my name. 'Otto, there is another reason for bringing you here. I need you to meet someone.'

FAMILIAR TERRITORY

He didn't tell me who and I didn't waste my breath asking, I just followed obediently as he expected.

Once outside again, he said, 'I am taking you to meet Carenis. If you are wondering who that is, the answer is that he is an ogre. There are a lot of them here though mostly they keep to themselves. I hired him and his brother because they are better at managing the shilt. The shilt will work with the demons but despise us because they know we are repulsed by them. The ogres have no such qualms. Carenis, like most ogres, has a limited ability with elemental magic. Mostly they use it to make weapons - Carenis also has an effective shield which is anchored to his body.'

'Why am I meeting him?'

'He will act as a go between for the shilt. Soon you will be travelling with them as you collect new familiars, but you killed rather a lot of them recently and they might try to kill you.'

'You want me to return to the mortal realm with shilt who might try to kill me? We both know how that will go for them.' I killed hundreds of them in Bremen when they attacked as a swarm. 'If I am forced to kill them, how will I return here?' I asked questions because I wanted to know how far Daniel had thought this through. I wanted to go back to Earth with the shilt at my side, my scratchy beginning of a plan depended on it.

'That is why Carenis will be there to manage the relationship. They would obey me, but I do not have the time to continue visiting the mortal realm. Some of the familiars are ready for trading, I must strengthen my position since your activities here have weakened it recently.' If his comment was aimed at making me feel regret, he misjudged.

'How many targets do I need to capture tonight?'

Daniel led me toward a clump of trees. 'None. If I try to manage too many at one time, it leads to problems. As the familiars get stronger, they fool themselves that they can band together to overwhelm me. More than a century ago, I learned to limit the number I hold and move them on before they get a chance to think.'

As we neared the trees, what I first thought was a boulder stepped into the moonlight.

'Ah, Carenis. I hope you have not been waiting too long,' said Daniel with unexpected politeness. 'This is my new familiar, Otto Schneider. Please introduce him to the hive leader as discussed.' Daniel stopped walking and turned to me. 'Once you are finished here, I want you to return to the warehouse and continue training the newest familiars. If you successfully move these on, I will grant you another visit to your wife.'

I needed more than occasional visits. She needed me to be there as much as possible. I kept my mouth shut about it because I knew telling him would only give him more leverage. Daniel had no interest in listening to what I might say, though, he had already walked away. I looked up at the enormous ogre and wondered quite how the next part of my evening was going to go.

Chapter 12

'You are quite sure it was the same man?'

'Demon,' Heike corrected. 'He is a demon, not a man, and yes, for the tenth time. When you get trapped in an alternate version of Earth and have to fight to survive only to then be told the only way home is by a demon granting you passage. You tend to remember the face of the demon.' She was trying to keep her tone even and her manner professional but Deputy Commissioner Bliebtreu kept asking the same damned questions and it was starting to really piss her off. 'Look, Otto Schneider was there and so was the demon. They appeared to be working together. I distinctly heard Otto shout for Daniel to open a portal right before they both vanished.'

'And you said that Otto is bound to the demon?' Bliebtreu confirmed, another question he had asked multiple times.

'That was the cost of our passage home. He killed Daniel's familiar, a wizard called Edward Blake, and Daniel forced Otto to replace him.'

'Now they are working together.'

Heike didn't think it was that simple. 'Otto wouldn't turn his back on us. Whatever he is doing, he must have a plan.'

'You don't know him that well,' argued Chief Muller, the only other person in the room.

'I know him well enough. He willingly sacrificed himself to save Katja Weber. He is with the demon now because he gave himself to save her. How many officers would do the same?'

Chief Muller continued to argue. 'You saw him agree to go with the one you call Daniel, but how do you know that wasn't a show put on to trick you?'

Heike swore. 'To what end? How could he possibly benefit?' She pushed herself upright and out of the chair. 'We are done here. I filed my report. Otto Schneider was at the hospital. They confirmed he visited his wife and was there for over an hour by himself. If he returns, they will call the station; I gave them the hotline number. I need to see my kids and I need some sleep.'

Bliebtreu barred her exit. 'If you have contact with Otto Schneider and don't tell me about it, I will have you arrested.'

His threat didn't go down well, Heike darting forward a metre to get into his face. 'If you ever threaten me again, you're going to have to arrest me.'

Chief Muller stepped between them. 'Okay, let's break it up. Bliebtreu, I can vouch for Lieutenant Dressler, she's as solid as they come.'

Heike didn't wait for Bliebtreu to say anything else; she wasn't interested in hearing it. She shoved her way past him and left the room.

Chief Muller pushed the door shut again. 'So tell me, Deputy Commissioner of a secret branch of the police, what is it that you propose to do about the supernatural creatures roaming this city and killing its citizens most nights?'

Chapter 13

Carenis took me to meet the shilt. I found it a little surreal. Every other time I had ever met them, they were trying to kill me, and, to be fair, not doing a very good job of it.

The ogre stood two and a half metres tall. There were two tusks protruding from his lower jaw which looked like it had been carved from a piece of granite. The only creature I had ever seen which might have been taller was Zachary when he transformed into a werewolf. The ogre was easily as wide as him, though, his shoulders, arms and legs bulging and thick with muscle. His face, in fact most of his exposed skin was covered in a thin fur but growing in the fur was moss and small plants and I saw small insects moving when I focussed on a single spot for long enough.

He didn't say much but I understood him when he spoke. 'The shilt will obey,' he rumbled, his voice possibly the deepest I had ever heard.

'That is what Daniel told me.'

'They know where to find humans with auras.'

'Helpful,' I agreed.

That was pretty much the extent of his conversation as he led me through some woods to reach a clearing. I looked around expecting to see shilt, but there was no one in sight.

Just as I got to the point where I felt I needed to prompt Carenis to tell me what we were waiting for, the small bush ahead of us moved. Branches folded to the side as a shilt emerged from the undergrowth.

'They live underground?' I asked.

The ogre turned his head my way and stared down at me, his forehead wrinkling in confusion at my question. 'They sleep underground. It is safe there.'

Safe from what I wondered but didn't ask. The bushes to my front covered a wider entrance than I realised at first; soon shilt were spilling from it half a dozen at a time until more than a hundred were facing me. They were devoid of the enchantments they wore to disguise themselves on Earth, and I know that it is considered incredibly racist to say they all looked the same to me, but they did. I could not tell one from the other. They were all the same height and their bodies were the same shape. Their reptilian skin covered their entire bodies; this was the first time I had seen them without clothes, but even that was the same shade and pattern.

To Carenis I whispered. 'How do I tell if I am talking to a boy shilt or a girl shilt?'

Again, Carenis gave me the confused look. 'They are neither. Shilt have one gender and reproduce by themselves.'

They were asexual? It made no difference to me, but it was something to remember. One of them stepped forward, its face turned up slightly as it sniffed the air.

'I am hive leader. Daniel has told us we must work with you now until the death curse fails. Only then can we kill you.'

'Ha!' A snort of laughter escaped my lips. 'Daniel told me you wouldn't hold a grudge.'

'He is wrong,' the hive leader replied evenly.

Carenis interrupted before the shilt and I could begin to discuss the future. 'You will select six shilt to act as escort to the mortal realm tomorrow,' his rumbling voice commanded.

The hive leader said, 'It was agreed.' Then it shifted its eyes from the ogre to me. 'What assurance do we have that they will return alive? The wizard has killed many of my hive and many from other hives. What will stop him doing so again?'

The ogre shifted his attention as well, staring down at me so I was the focus for all eyes. 'I give you my guarantee,' he rumbled. 'If the wizard harms any of them, I will kill him myself.'

That did it for the shilt. Reading shilt facial expressions is hard, imagine trying to work out if a cow is perplexed, but the hive leader looked not only surprised at the ogre's declaration, but pleased. 'That is sufficient,' it said. I guess they didn't know about my unique condition.

'What if one of them accidentally dies and their death was nothing to do with me?' I asked, thinking it likely I was going to kill them all sooner or later.

'None of them will come to harm, wizard,' Carenis stated as if predicting the future. 'I gave the hive leader my promise.' Bringing his face down so it was a few centimetres from mine, he made his threat clear. 'You will find me much harder to kill than a pack of shilt, wizard. It would be unwise to defy me.'

The shilt were already going back into their underground lair, the meeting was over so far as they were concerned. Carenis too was moving away. I would meet a six shilt escort a little less than twenty-four hours from now and be heading back to the mortal realm. Right now, it was already bedtime but there would be no sleep. I had familiars to train and though it would impress Daniel that I was putting so much effort into the task, I wasn't doing it for his benefit. I was doing it for them.

Chapter 14

Approaching the warehouse, I realised it was the first time I had seen it from the outside. Each time Daniel and I came and went, we did so via a portal. There were shilt guarding the exit; I guessed that to be their purpose anyway since they were hanging around outside and I couldn't see any other reason for their presence.

Approaching on foot they saw me from a long way off, wary eyes studying my approach. I slowed to make it obvious I intended to talk to them. 'What do you get from working with Daniel?' My question seemed to surprise them as if no one ever asked them anything or ever took an interest. I prompted them to answer. 'I mean, it's not as if you need wages and the work you do can be risky, lord knows I've killed plenty of your brethren when they were foolish enough to threaten people. So what is it?'

'There are promises,' one replied guardedly, answering my question but telling me nothing.

'Promises? What did Daniel promise? What is it that drives a shilt to put in an honest day's work?' I think my choice of phrase confused them, so I tried again. 'What is it that a shilt needs?'

'Sustenance,' the same shilt answered but one of his companions swatted his arm to shut him up.

Then the one who wanted the secrets kept said, 'We will be allowed to live. Daniel has it in his power to grant us freedoms other demons will not offer. He is among the highest demons, so he will be awarded a large territory to govern when the battle is done. That is why we work for him.'

I narrowed my eyes to squint at each of them in turn. They looked nervous. Perhaps that was just me and the threat I represented, but I thought it was something else. There was something hidden in their words and especially in the word sustenance. They fed on life energy, draining their victims to leave them dead. I would need to think on this and find someone to ask. Pushing past them, I entered the building to look for the captives inside. They were all in the wide area beyond the offices at the front and easy enough to find.

Coming through a door and onto the raised platform startled many of them, a sudden silence falling over the room as I disturbed it. They were formed into small clusters, ten men in one group on one side, half a dozen women in a group in the middle and other random groups. Many were practising their magic, but not all. Some were locked in discussion which reminded me of Daniel's comment about them banding together if left alone for too long.

Clearly wary of me, much like the shilt, they didn't know where my loyalties might lie. It was time to set that straight.

'Are there any demons here?' I asked, which got no replies but a lot of glances between the captives. 'Is there anyone in this room who is not a human torn from their home?' I had personally overseen the capture of every one of them, so what I was asking was whether they knew someone else was among them.

Finally, Ayla spoke, 'No, Otto. There is no one else here.'

She was in the group comprising only women, all of whom were aged between their mid-twenties and late thirties. I addressed the whole room, 'You're probably wondering whose side I am on and whether you can trust me.'

'You took us from our homes,' an American man pointed out. 'You made slaves of us.'

I nodded. 'Yes, I did that. I will assure you that I had no choice in the matter and that I did so not only under duress but with the knowledge that it was going to happen anyway.'

'Why should we believe you?' he demanded, suddenly spokesperson for the assembly.

I tried to remember his name. 'Mike, isn't it? From Connecticut. Your distrustful nature is natural in this environment. Daniel, my master, will soon begin to take you from here. You will be distributed to other demons and you will essentially be their slaves. Some may fare better than others and receive better treatment than others. There is nothing I can do to prevent this from happening.' I drew in a breath. 'However, I think there is a way that we can return home.'

I got a buzz of whispers in response and a dozen shouted questions as they wanted to know when, how soon, how, and why haven't I done it already?

I waved them to silence with my hands. 'Please,' I begged. 'I got here a day before the earliest of you, I just happen to know a bit more than you because I have fought Daniel before.'

'You told me you couldn't travel between the realms,' Ayla reminded me.

'That is correct, I cannot. But I have done so in the past by forcing a shilt to take me. On that occasion, I rescued about a dozen people.'

'So that is what you will do? Force one of those awful lizard things to take us home? What will stop them coming for us again the next night?' The question came from a Swiss woman.

I addressed her by name when I answered, 'Martha, that is precisely why I haven't attempted anything yet. If I were to send you home now, I would achieve nothing except to tip my hand. When we do this, I need to know that it will stick. I will train you shortly, show you more that you can do to defend yourselves.' That got another ripple of chatter because all they had been shown so far was how to manipulate air and water. Some were more advanced than that and were already able to conjure fire and two had taught themselves to move earth but only on a small scale. 'I cannot guess what is ahead of us but escaping this realm and returning to Earth in a way that ensures we are not immediately targeted again is my goal and should be yours too. I wish I could give you what you want now, but it is not in my power at this time. Be patient, play along, and be ready to fight because it may come down to that.'

It wasn't exactly a rousing speech, but it buoyed their spirits. None of them wanted to stay here, but I feared for how many I might actually be able to help. Once they were spread to other demons and bound to them, I had two additional problems to overcome. The first was how to break the binding. I felt certain it was possible because it was magical. If one can create a spell, the same spell can be undone. I just needed to work out how. Or perhaps I didn't. That was the problem with not having all the answers. If they were back in the mortal realm and hidden from the demons, would the binding lead the demons to them? Until I knew, I couldn't risk the escape.

There were questions from everyone, but the time I had with them was short and the need for them to learn how to use their skills for fighting too great. Their masters might employ them for mundane tasks such as heating water, but I wanted to teach them to explode a creature from the inside by superheating all its cells. One would make a bath the perfect temperature, the other might alter the course of a battle.

I made them practice for six hours.

Broken into small groups by ability, I had someone who had mastered a particular manipulation or conjuring help that group to learn it too. Everyone advanced at different speeds as one might expect, but everyone advanced. I really wanted to take the two who could perform earth spells outside so they could see what I could do. It wasn't to show off. I wanted them to see it so they would know what was possible. We couldn't for fear the shilt might see so as everyone tired, and I accepted that they would need some sleep, I had them clear an area in the back corner of the warehouse. It was well away from the raised platform where Daniel would always materialise or, if already in this realm, where he would enter, so I believed he would not see it.

Getting everyone to form a semi-circle around me, I said, 'I will demonstrate what is possible. You are all able to send heat into an object. Some have to be touching it to do that, but practice will improve your skills. Earth spells are among the most devastating when used effectively. In open ground you can upturn a swathe of land to bury your enemy.' I began reaching into the concrete floor to feel the atoms forming it. 'You can send a ripple across it to knock them from their feet.' Once I had an area about a metre in diameter, I began pushing heat into it. 'If you are strong enough, you can tear huge boulders from the ground and then use an air spell to throw them.' The effort made me sweat, but as I pushed yet more heat into my chosen spot, I knew it was nearing the critical point.

Someone pointed, the ground was beginning to glow.

'Or,' I announced triumphantly, 'you can create lava.' The concrete took on a shiny liquid look and a bubble rose to the surface like a hot mud spring. It popped and spat a glob of molten rock that almost hit my foot. I jerked back with a nervous laugh. 'The demons are powerful. Never fool yourself that they are not, but we are not without weapons of our own.'

The demonstration over, and the rock floor returning to a solid, if very hot, state now that I was no longer pushing heat into it, the crowd of captives edged forward to see. Some held their hands over the superheated concrete to see how close they could get them, and a young Japanese man ran across it to the sound of gasps and applause.

I hoped I had given them something to believe in tonight. They were trapped here, but it might not be forever. It wasn't just them though. If there were forty new familiars in this warehouse, how many were there in the immortal realm? How many wanted to escape? I believed the answer would be most of them, but I also feared that many may have fallen foul of Stockholm syndrome or had perhaps been offered reward for their loyalty which they now perceived to be more attractive than escape. Karen and Rita had been here with Daniel for one hundred and sixty years, were they too indoctrinated now? Would they want to escape if it was offered?

I was going to find out, but I would need to tread carefully.

As I began to back away, knowing there was nothing more I could do tonight, Ayla caught my arm. 'Otto, I think I know something that will help.'

Chapter 15

The first tranche of the new familiars was to be taken away this morning. It wouldn't be conducted in order of arrival, but in order of ability; those most capable getting selected first. After their training session last night and the conversation I had with them, the sense of terror for their future had not gone away, but they now held a slim glimmer of hope. Some of them didn't trust me, I couldn't blame them for that, but others, such as Ayla, believed me when I promised to do what I could to get them free.

Last night, or rather, in the early hours of this morning, I left them to sleep but would return with Daniel after breakfast, keen to be involved in the next stage of their lives here. Knowing where they were going was important, but I learned last night that most demons lived in a small area. Daniel let it slip when I asked him how he determined which familiar went to which demon.

For whatever reason, the demons found themselves in what would be Hampshire in England if this was actually Earth. Beelzebub was the sun around which they all orbited so when he settled there, the rest moved in around him. They could be anywhere; this was where they chose to be. Daniel, in an usually chatty mood, also explained why there were no children. When the death curse ripped them from one realm to deposit them in a new one, it also made them immortal. Perhaps the supreme being thought about his decision to leave the children behind, and perhaps he did not – no one got to ask him – but anyone under eighteen was left behind. The demons could not reproduce and could not die but the ultimate punishment was to have their children stripped from them and left to fend for themselves.

What became of them no one knew, but their similarity to humans in physiology and appearance meant they were probably absorbed into humanity and over time, their uniqueness was bred out. What happened to the demon children was a question that would continue to play on my mind for a long time.

Back at the warehouse, Daniel met other demons arriving there to be given their familiars. As I understood it, even after a century of stealing people from the mortal realm he still hadn't furnished the entire population but the demons operated a class system like the Indian caste hierarchy so demons such as Beelzebub and his inner circle were able to own multiple familiars before those near the bottom were allowed their first. Daniel had to rank and sort the familiars – one who might become powerful would not be permitted to stay with a lower ranking demon.

Attractiveness played a part too, which disturbed me. It suggested the familiars were also used for sex though I hadn't directly asked if that was the case yet. I didn't want to know. I couldn't do anything about it either way.

'Greetings, my friends,' Daniel acted like a television show host playing up to the crowd. There were ten demons, I counted, and I stiffened when one moved forward slightly to reveal Teague standing behind him. The short, balding demon had the appearance of a man in his sixties. I narrowed my eyes as he looked my way. I expected him to respond angrily to my presence; he and I were never going to get along. He smiled, though, which disturbed me. It suggested he knew something I didn't.

The first familiar to be called forward was Montrose. His skills had improved swiftly once he mastered a few simple spells. Glancing about, he advanced from the gaggle of captives huddled together for the false comfort it gave. Clearly scared, he still wore the clothes he wore when we took him, but he did his best to hide his terror.

'Bethusa, this is Montrose,' Daniel introduced the man. 'His skills are advancing; however, he will still require some training. For simple house tasks you will find him adequate, I am sure.'

Bethusa stepped forward to reveal herself. She was young and attractive, silky red hair falling in fine, straight lines to frame high cheekbones and the same piercing blue eyes all the demons had. Her face revealed how unimpressed she was with the tubby man appointed as her slave.

'Thank you, Daniel. I am grateful to finally have a familiar again.' The tone of her voice as she said the words did not reflect their content, but it matched the sour look on her face.

'Hold out your right hand,' Daniel instructed Montrose.

Montrose glanced at him and then at Bethusa and finally at me. He felt no desire to comply, however he knew what to expect and what the ritual involved because I took the time to explain it all to them last night. Bethusa pricked his thumb and pulled her dress down to reveal ninety percent of her left breast.

When Montrose failed to move, she growled at him, 'Place your thumb to my breast.' He did so quickly, a tiny flash of light visible under his digit as the binding sealed. When he pulled it away, her breast was marked with a red thumbprint that resembled a brand. Pulling her dress back into place, she murmured, 'Incensus.' Montrose dropped like a sack of rocks.

Behind him the other captives gasped. For many, this was the first time they had seen the power of the demons' binding in action.

'Incantus.' Bethusa reversed the spell, the second incantation returning power to Montrose's body. 'Just testing,' she said with a giddy giggle of pleasure. 'I would have preferred a girl, but a fat man will have to do until the death curse falls.' Montrose said nothing and didn't move when she turned around and began to walk away. Another growl from her got him moving, a last glance over his shoulder to his companions from the last week but then he was through the door and off to whatever life Bethusa had planned. He was armed with knowledge, and for now, that was the best I could do for him.

Daniel wasted no time in selecting the next familiar and then the one after that. The process of furnishing the first nine demons with their new slaves and binding them took less than an hour. Teague was the last. Throughout the process, he had been glancing my way and smiling, grinning to himself as much as to me. It was unnerving simply because I felt certain he was doing it because he had a nasty surprise in store. I wasn't wrong.

'Ayla,' Daniel called.

I drew in a sharp breath. 'No.'

Daniel snapped his eyes across to me. 'Be quiet, Otto.'

I closed the distance between us so I could whisper urgently, 'You cannot give her to Teague. He will abuse her to punish me.'

Daniel nodded. 'Yes, I expect so. You have no say in this, Otto. In fact, you have yourself to blame for her selection.' Upon seeing my angry, but questioning look, he explained, 'You will remember my promise to Teague on the snow-covered lawn of Katja Weber's house – I would provide him with a superior familiar.'

I remembered. 'She is not superior, Daniel. Her spell casting is one of the weakest here.'

Daniel didn't argue. 'Teague requested that I give him the familiar you showed the most interest in. That she is also very attractive helps immensely. Teague is a senior demon who has killed three familiars in the last century. He will not treat her well, Otto. This may upset you, but there is nothing you can do about it. Now stand down or must I exercise my dominion over you?'

My rage level made my head feel like it was a volcano. Pressure was building up inside and soon it was going to blow in a fashion so spectacular Daniel would wish he had died long ago. This was not the time and I knew it.

Forcing a polite nod of my head, I stepped back and let it happen - I let Daniel give sweet Ayla to that monster. I caught her eye as he bound her; she was terrified, her legs shaking with fear and rightfully so for the moment it was done, he whipped out a tendril of energy from his right hand. Daniel had used the same thing on me in a men's restroom in Magdeburg a week ago, but where he used it to torture me, Teague sent it to wrap around her throat like a dog lead, then yanked her from the room as she cried out in pain behind him and hurried to keep up.

'More of you will meet your new masters tomorrow,' Daniel shouted to quell the frightened chatter from the remaining captives. 'Continue practising.'

FAMILIAR TERRITORY

It was a terrible threat against which there was no defence. Under his gaze, they quickly started spreading out and forming into groups as they knew to do. As the air spells and other conjurings began, Daniel snapped around to glare at me. 'You still dare to challenge me, Otto?'

I had no response for him. None that he would like. Our entire relationship was predicated upon him having total control and me not being able to fight back. My obedience wasn't through choice, but through lack of choices. To make a point, I said, 'You keep giving me incentive to resist.'

'Yet you cannot resist,' he pointed out. 'I will not allow it, and should you attempt it I will punish you further. I treated you as equally as I could when I allowed you to visit your wife. I have nothing to benefit by doing so again. You must incentivise me, Otto, not the other way around. Please me with your actions, with your successes for me, and your life here might become tolerable.'

I think it was at this point that my masterplan began to change.

Chapter 16

The next two days passed in a blur of training sessions and familiar adoption ceremonies, as I came to think of them. It was as fitting a name as anything else. Soon there was only a handful of the familiars left and the cycle would repeat again.

I behaved and obeyed Daniel's instructions, but his need to engage with other demons kept him busy which gave me time by myself. Time which I used to explore.

Most familiars seemed to have little purpose. They were a status symbol, a reminder of the old times. Back when the demons ruled the planet, they used familiars as slaves to perform mundane functions for them. Fetching water, starting fires, cleaning and cooking, perhaps even catching or gathering the food. None of that was necessary now. Instead, their purpose was to fight with the demon when the death curse finally ends. They would be mortal again and vulnerable, but the familiars could be forced, via their binding and an incantation, to defend their demon master with their life. This was why they wanted familiars with strength. Those who could wield elemental magic in a dangerous way, me for instance, were of more value.

On the third day, as I made my way overland to the warehouse from Daniel's house, where I was now able to snatch a few hours of sleep each day, Sean McGuire appeared. He had been standing out of sight behind a thick tree trunk, swinging into view when I was almost on top of him.

'Top of the morning,' he hallooed.

FAMILIAR TERRITORY

Refusing to show my surprise at his sudden appearance, I replied, 'Good morning.' A natural urge to be guarded conflicted with my desire to find familiars who could help me. Sean might be one of them, but I would have to broach the subject carefully until I knew how loyal he felt to his master. If the demons ever found out what I planned, I couldn't imagine what they might do to me. However, I needed information, and some familiars had been here a long time. Was Nathaniel's slave one of them?

Sean was smiling beneath his hood. 'I wanted to catch up with you, Otto. I felt it necessary to discuss the lightning bolt you hit me with.'

Was that what this was? Did he bear a grudge and carry a need for retribution? 'I'm sorry I hit you,' I told him honestly. 'You were not my target and I was merely defending myself.'

He waved a hand of surrender. 'Oh, I'm not sore about it, Otto. That's what I came to tell you. In fact, I wanted to say it was a mighty fine piece of conjuring in such a short space of time. I'm not sure I could have done better. It really rattled my bones.'

'Thank you.' I nodded my head. 'I apologise, nevertheless. Will you walk with me? I need to get to the warehouse.'

Sean fell in next to me as I started walking again. 'Daniel giving away more familiars today, eh? That must be interesting work for you.'

I cocked an eyebrow. 'Kidnapping innocent people and turning them into slaves? Interesting is not a word I would choose.'

Sean pushed out his lips to show he conceded the point. 'There is another way you can look at it.'

'Oh, yes?'

'You are saving them. In the mortal realm they will most likely die when the demons return. My master, Nathaniel, tells me humanity have overrun the planet and like an infestation, must be purged. There is nothing on Earth, no weapon in the mortal realm that can prevent the demons from sweeping all before them when the death curse fails.'

Sensing a chance to gain information, I asked a question. 'How many demons are there?'

Sean chuckled. 'How many? A lot. A hundred thousand maybe. They don't all live here abouts, just the vast majority. It's not the number that will make the difference, it is the firepower they bring to bear. Mortal weapons can hurt them in theory, but I saw your shield, the demons can deploy similar defences. I have mine woven into my coat, so I have no need to activate it ever.'

Creating an argument so he would continue to reveal information, I said, 'A hundred thousand demons against seven billion humans? They have nuclear weapons. No shield will protect them against that kind of firepower. Cluster bombs, land mines, chemical weapons, these weapons may be evil, but humanity will deploy every last one of them to secure their survival.'

Sean chuckled again. 'It's not just the demons, Otto. Trust me when I say you are on the winning side. The demons will sweep the armies of humanity aside just as easily as they will the angels when they join the fray to stop them.'

'Where are the angels?' I asked. 'Why do they not prevent or deter Daniel from taking familiars?'

'There're too few of them. The demons outnumber them by as many as twenty to one. Like the demons, I do not know the true number, but they stand alone, no other magical races will rally to their side.'

'Why not?'

'Because they offer nothing. The angels want peace and harmony and for all races to prosper evenly. Each race wants to fight for their own rights and that is what the demons offer. They will let the shilt farm humans. They will allow the ogres to find their own land and banish all other races from it. Beelzebub is guaranteed the creatures of this realm will fight on his side.'

'The shilt will farm humans? You mean like cattle? Farm them for food?'

Sean nodded. 'Exactly like that. That is how it used to be I am told. How is it any different from humans farming cattle, or sheep, or anything. I heard a story from another familiar a few years back about humans keeping chickens in permanently lit buildings so they would never sleep and thus lay more eggs. They would live short lives and suffer every day just so there were enough eggs to go around. The shilt will feed on the humans they farm but never kill any of them. With a constant supply of sustenance, they don't need to kill their food source. Doesn't that sound better than farming a thing to death?'

It was impossible to argue against him, but that didn't mean I could let it happen. 'What do you think, Sean? Would you escape if you could? Would you return to the mortal realm and be free?'

'Ha!' he laughed. 'I swear, Otto, you didn't listen to a word I said. The demons will win. Anyone on their side will benefit, even the familiars. Nathaniel will grant me my own territory within his kingdom. I hope it is somewhere warm. Escape is not possible, and if it were, your master would come for you the moment the sun fell.'

I had broached the subject of Sean leaving and his position was clear. There were thousands of familiars here, I knew that from Daniel. How many of them felt like Sean was something I needed to be careful finding out.

Chapter 17

'You were right, master.'

Nathaniel nodded. It was as he expected, and it was good news. 'You believe he continues to resist Daniel's commands?'

'It felt as if he were trying to recruit me, master.'

'To what end?'

'My impression was that his end goal is escape.'

Nathaniel's eyes showed his surprise, but it quickly turned to mirth. 'Escape,' he laughed. 'He cannot travel between the realms and cannot break his binding. Even if he could convince a shilt, a demon, or any other creature to transport him, there is nowhere he can go where Daniel would not find him.' Nathaniel could sense the opportunity beckoning. Daniel taunted him with his success. Still his underling and from a lower caste, Daniel had ascended in the last few hundred years and his popularity among the population threatened to eclipse Nathaniel's position. Were it another demon, one Nathaniel had no history with, he might not care, but Daniel chose to rub his success in Nathaniel's face. Now there existed a chance to return him to his rightful place at the bottom of the pile.

Seeing the plan form in his head, Nathaniel nodded to himself. 'I have a task for you, Sean. You might call it a mission, in fact.'

FAMILIAR TERRITORY

'What is your bidding, master?' Sean waited obediently to be given instruction. Were it not for the demons, he would have died as a starving young man in Ireland, barely subsisting on a diet deficient in the nutrients a person needed to survive. Remaining in Ireland and living long enough to find a wife, he could expect to watch his children die as the British denied their Irish farmers the right to have enough to live by. Instead, he lived far beyond his expected lifespan and would be rewarded when the earth was reclaimed. He would do anything Nathaniel asked.

'I want you to make friends with Daniel's new familiar. Join him, help him, organise a revolution if that is what it takes. I want Daniel to fall from grace in the most impressive manner possible. Otto Schneider must create havoc here. See that he does.'

'Yes, master.'

Chapter 18

When the fourth set of familiars were given to their new masters like new puppies being handed out once weaned from their mother, I was set to repeat the cycle. That would start tonight but I would go without Daniel, a small detachment of shilt travelling with me instead. They would identify where the likely familiar lived and bring me back and forth between the realms. Capture was down to me. I cannot say I was happy about it.

The first set of familiars, the first forty I aided Daniel to take, were now all spread among the demon community, but thanks to Ayla, we were able to communicate. She took a secret code from her childhood and taught it to everyone in the group. She used it as a little girl to pass messages between her friends that their parents and siblings could not decipher and would most likely ignore if they ever saw it. Now, it was to be employed on their demon masters. It was simple, but no less ingenious for it.

Because we didn't know where anyone had gone, each of the new familiars placed a symbol in the front window of their house. It was a circle with an arrow, a bit like a cupid's heart. If the house was set back from the road, they would find a way to leave a marker in the street outside. This way we could find where they lived. Then a second symbol, this time a pair of dots, told whether the demon was home or not. In total there were only twenty-six symbols to memorise; an easy task but it provided a secret language we could communicate with.

I wouldn't need to track them all down, I could rely on the new familiars to find each other, but I needed to know where enough of them were so that I could get messages to them, check their status and arrange meetings if such a thing were possible. Travelling to the warehouse this morning, I saw two houses displaying the tiny symbols. Both had a pair of dots next to the circle and arrow to let me know it wasn't safe to approach. When I passed again and found the dots gone, I would find out which of the new familiars lived there.

Right now, with no one watching me, and Daniel believing I would be resting before tonight's excursion, I went to the one house I did know; the only house other than Daniel's I had been inside and could identify: Teague's.

He had Ayla, and I felt a need to check on her, though I recognised the folly of my visit. Unless she reported he was a pleasure to live with, which I doubted he was, I would be yet more angry at my inability to stop or prevent the abuse the demons handed out. Sure, I could attack Teague again, but it would undo everything I had achieved so far and once recovered, Teague would exact revenge on Ayla. It was a lose/lose situation for me.

His house was quiet when I approached, my eyes searching for the symbol in a window. Like many other houses the demons chose to inhabit here, his was set back from the road with a sweeping driveway leading to it. It was the kind of house that would cost a lot on Earth. The symbol wasn't in a window, it had been chalked onto the path in front of the house ... and there were no dots.

I ran to the door, hammering on it without care until it opened. Ayla's face appeared as she opened the door, answering questions about her treatment instantly as I took in the black eye and fat lip. She took one look at me and burst into tears. Then she reached for me in need of human comfort and I kicked the door closed as I held her to my chest.

I didn't bother to coo at her or lie that it was going to be alright. We were slaves in a terrible place and unable to protect ourselves from the indignities we suffered. After half a minute, she pushed herself away and wiped at her face, apologising for her outburst.

'I'm sorry, Otto. It is good to see you. Have you been able to speak with anyone else?'

I shook my head. 'No. I have nothing to tell them yet. Are there any other familiars in this house? Have you seen anyone else?'

'Teague doesn't let me out. At least, he hasn't yet and threatened terrible things if he catches me leaving the house.'

'Does he punish you out of spite?' I swear I didn't want to know the answer, but I asked it anyway.

Ayla bit her lip. 'It will do no good to talk about it. Just know that I will kill myself if I stay here. I am all in with you to find a way to escape.'

The sound of a door closing in another part of the house made our eyes widen in fear: Teague was home.

There was no time for talk, I grabbed the door handle and let myself out, Ayla quickly kissing my cheek in thanks as I fled the house and slipped away. I didn't want to read anything into the kiss. She was a married woman with children, but I couldn't deny that it stirred my soul. I hadn't felt the warmth of a woman's touch in most of a year now, my own wife unable to give me any comfort. Since seeing her in the hospital a few days ago, I tried to focus on not thinking about her, but Kerstin's face filled my mind when I slept. She needed me now more than ever. She moved her head. It might be nothing, but it might be the start of her waking up and the doctor wanted me to spend time with her. If I were not trapped here, my every moment would be in her company as I tried to help her find a way back to me.

Realising my thoughts were a spiral that might lead me to depression and would at least rob me of the focus I needed to succeed here, I banished the unwelcome images from my head and hurried onward. I didn't get far.

I intended to take a meandering route back to Daniel's house so I could look at more houses and find more of my new familiars. No more than twenty metres from Teague's place I was stopped short by eyes watching me.

A man and a woman were in the woods that separated the houses. They left their hiding place as soon as they saw me spot them. They were both in their twenties, though that would be the age they were frozen at, not their true age. I could tell they were human just by bringing up my second sight. It showed me their auras and the link to the ley lines in the ground which the demons did not have. It was a thin wisp of golden thread because they were not consciously pulling on the line, and that told me their intention, whatever it might be, was most likely friendly.

I waited on the road for them. The man led, the woman trailing close behind. He was stick thin, but not gaunt which is to say I thought him to be well-nourished but naturally lean. He wore cargo pants beneath a thick winter coat but like all the familiars I saw, it was old and tatty.

When he got within five metres, he started to talk. 'You are the one who killed Edward Blake.' He made it a statement and my hackle went up as I sensed anger in his voice. Had I killed his friend?

If the pair planned to attack me, they had better have brought their A game. I drew in ley line energy as I lifted my hands ready for battle. 'What of it?' I demanded as I conjured the atoms around me. Lightning was fast and destructive and neither of my opponents were ready for it.

The man stopped in his tracks when he saw the threat I presented. Score one for the mighty German! Fear me mortals and quake in fear.

'What are you doing?' the man asked.

The woman peered around his back. 'We came to thank you.' Both looked at me with open expressions, nothing hidden in their faces and I could tell they were telling me the truth. Feeling dumb now with my hands raised and a small storm swirling above my head, I twitched, accepted they intended me no harm and let the power in my spell dissipate naturally on the wind.

I said, 'Sorry. I thought maybe he was a friend of yours.'

The man's eyebrows rose to the top of his head and he burst out laughing. 'You won't find many here who were his friends. He is responsible for bringing most of us here. Gwyneth and me, I'm Tiberius, we were taken on the same night in 1947. He was a ruthless git, that Edward Blake let me tell you. I am here to shake your hand.' Tiberius advanced to do just that. Gwyneth following him and doing the same.

I noticed they both wore rings. 'Are you married?' I asked.

He looped his hand into hers with a glance at her face. 'As close as we can be here. I would say we were never joined before God in a church, but, of course, there is no God, just Godfrey and Beelzebub.'

'He means yes,' Gwyneth clarified. 'We consider ourselves married though our respective masters have no idea.'

Tiberius's face turned serious. 'I met a familiar last night at the duel. A woman called Martha.' The one I took from Bern in Switzerland, another young mother. 'She talked of returning home. You have a plan, don't you?'

His question shocked me. Yes, I had an intention to escape. It would be wrong to call it a plan because that suggested I knew how I might do it, but the new familiars, the ones I felt responsible for and wanted to return with me, were sworn to secrecy. Martha had blabbed in less than a day.

Tiberius and Gwyneth stared at me with open hopeful faces. I could test them swiftly enough. 'What is it that you are asking me?' I made sure I sounded guarded. If the demons already caught scent of my intentions and sent these two to trap me, I was giving nothing away.

However, Gwyneth didn't hesitate to say, 'If there's an escape plan, we want to be part of it.'

Her words rang with truth. I pointed to Tiberius. 'I want to hear what you want.'

'The same thing. My master has little use for me, my life here is not so terrible as some because he ignores me most of the time. Tell me though, how do you propose to break the binding?'

He too was telling the truth. The words I whispered in secret to the new familiars had already found its way into the community of familiars. These were dangerous times. His question hit on one of two problems I faced. The first I believed I could get around; this was the bigger issue.

FAMILIAR TERRITORY

I explained my logic. 'It is magical. Magic obeys a set of rules and that which is done can be undone. It is all about power. The death curse has resisted reversal because it was cast by the strongest among their race and he used his dying breath to deploy it. Giving your life to weave a spell must add layers of reinforcement, but it is fading with time. A binding has to follow the same set of rules.'

'Bindings can be transferred,' said Gwyneth helpfully. The comment was aimed at her husband, the effect intended to make him consider the possibility that I might have a point.

It also gave me something to latch onto. 'If they can be transferred between demons then they are not permanent. Do you not know of anyone who has ever explored the concept of freeing themselves?'

They exchanged a grim look. 'Even talking about it as we are is punishable by death,' Tiberius admitted fearfully. 'The demons sustain us with their blood, which means we never age. The only way anyone has ever escaped is by taking their own life.'

Gwyneth added, 'There have been a lot of people we met here who chose that option. Some demons are terribly cruel. Others anger their masters and get killed by them. One blast of hellfire and poof; you're gone.'

Tiberius frowned as he remembered something. 'The other new familiar we met yesterday, what was his name?'

Gwyneth supplied the answer, 'Montrose.'

'Yes, Montrose,' Tiberius echoed. 'He told a fanciful tale about you getting hit by hellfire more than once and getting up each time.

I nodded, sensing an opening. 'I killed Teague a while back, blowing him up from the inside by heating the water inside his cells to boiling point.' Their eyes went wide in disbelief at my claim. 'I captured a shilt in the mortal realm and forced him to bring me and a companion here to rescue some people Edward Blake took. Teague came back, of course, his body reforming immediately after it exploded, but something happened when he burst, and I absorbed a dose of demon magic.' They were going to ask me how that worked so I said, 'I cannot explain it in detail, but I have demon blood in my veins now and I am immortal, not just immune to hellfire.'

'Immortal,' breathed Gwyneth, her voice a hushed whisper. 'Like the demons?'

I nodded. 'Trust me on this. Daniel has tried to kill me many times. I fell into an exploding diesel tanker with a werewolf whose claws were puncturing my chest and I had my right hand almost burned off when I conjured a lake of lava to kill a small army of shilt. If I can do all that by myself, we can break a binding between us. We just need to work out how.'

They were silent for several seconds, letting the idea flood into their imaginations. When they turned inwards to look at each other, I said, 'We need to keep this quiet. The more people know about what we are planning, the more likely it is that the demons will learn of our treachery and stop us.' Their eyes showed fear as they imagined that event. 'However, if we can work out a way to break the binding, all we need is a way home and I have shilt at my command.'

I didn't think I could just order a shilt to open a portal but there was no need to share that with them at this time. I would work out the travel plans later, and there was an inkling of a plan for it already itching away at the back of my head – something I wanted to try out.

My new friends, as I chose to think of them had a look that said they didn't want to dare believe the possibility of my suggestion. It was too fantastic, too desirable, like being told you can win the lottery and you don't even have to buy a ticket, just perform a task.

'Do we talk to Byron?' asked Gwyneth, the question aimed at Tiberius.

Throwing my hands in the air as they instantly defied the concept of keeping our secret, secret, I asked, 'Who's Byron?'

Chapter 19

Heike was staring at a picture of Otto's face. It arrived on her desk a few minutes ago, the Alliance circulating it to those they were working with in Bremen. His face was on the news already, plastered there because he made the top ten most wanted in America.

She found it hard to take in, but it seemed he had switched sides. Two weeks ago, he risked his life to rescue her from demons and other awful creatures after Edward Blake broke into her house with a pack of shilt and took her against her will. She fought and kicked and almost got to her gun, but they dragged her through a portal anyway. Hopelessly trapped, it was Otto who came for her. Her and others, including the teenage girl, Katja Weber who Daniel stole from her parents just the previous night.

Now there were pictures of Otto with Daniel caught on house security cameras in seven different homes in America plus three across Europe and one in England. One of the people he took was the daughter of a politician, a young woman with two small kids called Ayla Pendragon. Her father was Deputy Secretary of the Treasury, or something like that. Whoever he was, he had enough clout to have the FBI looking for Otto.

It didn't take long after his face hit the television screens and internet feed for the Alliance in Germany to identify him. The American Alliance wanted him captured. Supernatural or not, I guess no one gets to kidnap a politician's daughter.

If he had replaced Edward Blake as Daniel's lackey, or if he hadn't, he was clearly involved at some level, and the Alliance planned to catch him. Carrying the photograph in her head, she knocked on the office door assigned to Deputy Commissioner Bliebtreu. This was his third day at the station, his taskforce patrolling the streets at night in their armoured vehicles having little effect on whether the shilt showed up or not. To date they had proven just as ineffective as the police in stopping the creatures disguised as humans from attacking. That was what brought her to be knocking on the door.

'Come.' Bliebtreu's voice echoed out through the closed door. He had been talking on the phone, his conversation too indistinct for her to make out but she had chosen to wait until it ended before knocking. She opened the door and went inside, closing it behind her.

Bliebtreu was sitting on the edge of his desk, perched there to make the phone call with his mobile still in his hand. His eyes asked the question – what do you want?

'I wish to join the SIA,' Heike announced, forcing herself to speak calmly rather than blurt as she took the first step in trashing a career she had worked so hard for her entire adult life.

Her announcement got the deputy commissioner's attention. He stood and came around the desk to extend his hand to hers. As they shook, he said, 'Welcome on board.'

Chapter 20

On the same day that I was to begin stealing people from Earth by myself, things began to fall into place. Not that I would claim to have a masterful strategy and feel assured of victory, but I was no longer alone and that meant I could slowly begin to build toward the end goal I perceived.

Tiberius and Gwyneth took me to meet Byron, explaining along the way that their masters – a term given to both male and female demons from the familiar's perspective – were part of a fore-guard in Beelzebub's forces. They had been training with their masters for many years in battle tactics. There were demons, Nathaniel was one of them he learned, who were essentially soldiers. They had not been before the death curse; there had been no need, but their battles with the angels following the curse and their incarceration here, identified some who possessed a military mind.

The familiars understood the role they were to play, that of a human shield. In practice they stood in front of their masters, controlled by them through the binding and forced to protect their demon with their life if necessary.

It explained why Daniel claimed demand for familiars was stepping up – everyone wanted one. Or more than one, probably. One might think Daniel would recruit more and more to help him identify and capture the familiars, but I got the distinct impression he didn't really trust anyone. If they learned to do what he could do, they might weaken his position, not strengthen it. It seemed short-sighted yet reflected what I had seen; the demons were not unified. By their nature they were divisive.

I listened intently to Tiberius and Gwyneth, learning constantly and understanding why they wanted to leave their masters. Even if Sean was right about the demons winning, I would rather die on the right side, than be on the advancing line against my own people.

They also explained who Byron was. He was the first familiar. Not first as in first among equals, but the one who had been here longest.

We found him lounging on a rock high on a hill with a marvellous view over the rolling countryside. There were two other familiars with him who Tiberius introduced as Chen and Meilin. The two women were Chinese by birth, their petite bodies and jet-black hair stark against Byron who had red hair, stood a head taller than me and was broad like an ox.

Upon being introduced, I extended my hand. Byron stopped lounging and got up to shake it. 'I'm not the first, actually,' he corrected Tiberius who had made the introduction. 'Not by a long way,' he assured me, but those who had come before had all been killed when they could not reach a skill level the demons found acceptable.

'I am a Viking,' he announced proudly. It produced eye rolls from his two female companions who were clearly used to his bragging.

'Otto is bound to Daniel,' explained Tiberius, speaking for me.

'Ah,' said Byron. 'The one who killed Edward Blake. He had it coming, I suppose. You have already begun to supply new familiars in his stead, though, so little has changed from my perspective.'

I didn't want to dwell on what I was doing; I would learn nothing talking about myself. To break the ice, I asked him what happened to the familiars who were here before him.

'They are all dead and in many ways that is my fault,' he admitted sadly. 'I was impressed by myself, by my skills once they developed, so I showed off. The demons with familiars then saw how weak their own familiars were and killed them. They wanted ones like me, you see?'

Byron came from Norway and though he bore the appearance of a nineteen-year-old with a touch of fluff not yet stubble on his chin, he was over three hundred years old. He had been here that long, and it meant he knew more than most.

He belonged to Beelzebub, the demon king forcing his original master to transfer ownership when he learned of the young Viking wizard's power. Chen and Meilin both belonged to one of Beelzebub's generals. 'There are six,' Byron explained. 'Nathaniel, Acadus, Bitrius, Martha, Aksel, and Berthilda. Each of them commands an army for Beelzebub with lieutenants to control different factions within the army. They have been gearing up for the fight to retake Earth for a long time.' I had no doubt this was important information but none of it meant anything until we escaped.

Gwyneth said, 'Otto has a question about the binding. He wants to break it.'

Byron tuned his head to look at me. It was a slow, lazy move, one which a person might reserve for someone who had a stupid idea. Settling back onto his rock as he looked to the view beyond, he said, 'That has never been done and don't think others haven't tried it.'

Nothing was going to put me off. 'Tell me how it works, Byron and what can be done. I am given to understand demons can transfer a binding from one to another.'

He nodded. 'They can. It is how I came to be Beelzebub's familiar. Also, a demon can release a binding, but I have only seen it happen once. The free familiar in that instance was set free so she could be killed by a creature called a whyker.'

'What's a whyker?' asked Meilin, interrupting Byron's flow but with a question I wanted an answer to.

Byron shifted position on his rock. 'It was about two-hundred years ago. The demons started getting excited about something called a whyker. Of course, I had no idea what it was, but it's an ancient creature the demons thought they had hunted to extinction several millennia ago. Like a giant scorpion but without the claws and stinger tail, it is a huge beast that sucks the life force from its victims much like the shilt but would attack and kill a demon given the chance. I don't think it could hurt the demons here, but they wanted it dead anyway and used a woman called Hayley as bait. Her master took her out to a vast plain of open ground and undid the binding that controlled her. She was free to go, he said. I think she was bewildered by it, but not for long because the whyker attacked her shortly after. While it was sucking her dry, the demons attacked. It still took a lot of them to subdue and then overpower it.'

'You were there?' I asked.

He nodded. 'I was. The whyker can shift forms which makes it hard to find and harder to kill, but they managed it eventually. The point, of course, is that a demon can release a binding.'

'They can also hold multiple bindings,' said Chen. 'Meilin and I have the same master and there are demons here with four or five familiars. The more they have, the greater their status provided their familiars are recognised as capable. Each of the generals has three or more.'

'Except Nathaniel,' Byron pointed out. 'He keeps just one, but Sean is probably the most dangerous wizard here.'

'How so?' I wanted to know.

Byron shrugged. 'The strength and power of his spells. His speed.'

'You know this because of duels he has fought for Nathaniel?' I sought to clarify.

Byron nodded his head. 'Yes. I fought him myself once so I can testify to his ability. I was one of the lucky ones.' I didn't understand what he meant but seeing me tilt my head in question, he continued to explain. 'What you saw last night was tame. Neither familiar really wanted to hurt the other, the injuries they inflicted were because they had no choice. They are friends, in fact. When Sean fights, all the demons attend because they are so keen to see who he will kill next. He is responsible for most of the deaths by duel in the last century. So, like I said, I was one of the lucky ones.'

He fell silent for a short while but spoke before anyone else could. 'I would not go so far as to state that it is his fault they die each time. I think Nathaniel encourages him to be ruthless, but …' he paused for a moment to consider what he wanted to say, 'I also think he enjoys it. Most of us are wise enough to fear him.'

This was interesting. Very interesting, in fact, but I wanted to get back to the subject at hand. I had no desire to test myself or prove myself, and there would be no need to if we could escape instead. Getting their attention, I said, 'Bindings can be freely exchanged or simply ended, and a demon can hold multiple bindings at any time. I think I can get us back to the mortal realm.'

Meilin and Chen acted as if startled by my statement, but Byron's almost-bored look didn't change. 'You plan to force one of the shilt to take you, yes?'

I found my eyes narrowing themselves at his attitude. 'That is one option but I am exploring others.' It was mostly a lie because I wasn't exploring at all. I had an idea to investigate but no clue whether it might work. 'Do you wish to remain here, Byron,' I asked, offering him a yes/no question so we could establish his position and move on.

He ducked the answer. 'It is not so simple as whether I want to stay or not. A chicken may want to fly, but if it is beyond it to do so, why waste time and effort on the fantasy?'

'But a chicken could climb high and achieve something close to flying,' argued Meilin which not only sounded better coming from her but was also better than the response waiting on my lips.

'What she said,' I agreed. 'The question,' I pressed him, 'is whether you wish to do nothing and remain here until the death curse breaks so you can then play a part in the genocide of mankind. Or whether, like me, you wish to do something about it. How many familiars are there here?' I asked as an insane idea popped into my head.

Chen said, 'Too many to count.'

'Thousands?' I asked.

'Certainly.' No one argued with her assessment.

I exhaled a breath through my nose. The opportunity was undeniable. 'Are you familiar with a man called Spartacus?' I asked.

Byron, a three-hundred-year-old man from Norway with no formal education had no idea what I was talking about, but the others did. The leader of a massive slave rebellion in ancient Rome, he banded together an army with nothing to lose and tore through Rome slaughtering countless masters along the way.

'Spartacus lost,' Gwyneth pointed out.

I couldn't escape the truth of it. 'And so might we. But I owe it to friends and family on Earth to try, and if we manage to escape, we can strike a blow that might set the demons reeling.'

Byron sat forward. 'Tell me more about this Spartacus.'

Chapter 21

The portal closed behind me with a barely audible pop. I was back in the mortal realm, this time with six shilt to accompany me. They were my transport, as I could not cross between realms by myself, but they were also my guides and very probably my chaperones. I had a distinct plan for tonight and how I wanted it to go. Unintentionally recruiting help earlier today enabled my loose ideas to take a little bit of form. I could almost call them a plan now. Getting to the end goal required many steps plus some fast work.

Having to retrieve new familiars for Daniel was an unavoidable distraction but one I could take advantage of. When one of the shilt placed its hand on my shoulder to steer me, I shrugged it loose and moved away from him. 'Touch me again and I'll kill you.'

Its lips peeled back in what I believed was supposed to be a smile but was impossible to interpret with its reptilian face. 'Then how will you get home?'

'There are six of you,' I pointed out. 'I need but one to open the portal.'

The smile faltered and faded, replaced by what was unquestionably an angry grimace. 'Daniel insisted we cooperate with you,' it growled unhappily. 'Our reward for working with Edward Blake and guiding him to and from the immortal realm was the chance to feed while we are here.'

I knew what it was asking. They intended to prey on the family of the persons I was here to target. Take the intended victim and let the shilt dispose of the family. Not on my watch. 'That will be a distraction.' The shilt all stopped moving to glance at each other and then at me. I made it look as if I was relenting. 'If you assist me to gather the familiars, I promise you will get your reward at the end.'

The shilt spokesman, since it appeared to have appointed itself as such, argued, 'At the end? Once we have taken five familiars back to the immortal realm, only then will you allow us to feed? One household will not sustain the six of us.'

I made it look like I was listening and nodded along as he complained. 'I'll tell you what. Why don't you tell me why it is that humans cannot open a portal? I consider that information of value. Tell me that and I will turn tonight into a feast.'

Their mood instantly buoyant, the shilt now looked excited. However, their spokesman tilted its head to look at me before it answered. 'The information will not help you. A human cannot open a portal because their skin is wrong. Ogres cannot open portals either. Many creatures cannot. In fact, very few races can.'

I pressed for more information. 'What is it about your skin that makes it possible. I heard it was a shilt who was the first to find a way through to the mortal realm.'

Having said it as a compliment, which caught them a little off guard since we were not on the same side, the shilt nonetheless sounded proud when it replied, 'It was a shilt. They discovered the linkage in the ley lines. The realms are separate but the energy that travels though the ground here also travels there; the two realms are linked by the lines …'

'So with an incantation, one can open a portal between the two realms?'

'You are fishing for information you do not need, wizard. We were warned to be wary of you.' The shilt's demeanour changed, becoming all business when a moment before it was almost congenial.

I smiled warmly. 'Yes, of course. Let's get to work. Which house are we targeting first?'

We were in a street in a European-looking city, but we could have been anywhere. I came through the portal to find myself in a street. I told the shilt I didn't want to materialise inside a child's bedroom, so we didn't. However, until I heard someone speak, I was going to have no way of knowing which continent we were on.

FAMILIAR TERRITORY

The house they led me to was a large detached place built over three stories – a town house. There were dozens of them to its left and right and more behind us on the other side of the street. There were trees lining the road, and as I passed between two cars to get to the pavement, I saw a number plate and realised that was how I could tell where I was.

We were in France. One of the big cities I thought given the skyline, but I couldn't see the Eiffel Tower poking up, so it probably wasn't Paris.

'Arriving in the street makes no sense,' the shilt complained to me as we approached the house. 'We will make noise breaking in and alert the humans. You can already see the one you need?'

It was asking if I could see the aura of magic, which I could, an indistinct glow on the second floor with a thin line burrowing down and into the ground beneath the house where it connected to a ley line deep underground.

'Too late now,' I replied as we neared the front door. It was raised up from street level by three concrete steps bordered by railing on both sides. I didn't finesse the lock open carefully by drawing moisture into it for freezing, I pulled my face into a grimace and let loose with a lightning bolt that obliterated the lock and killed the door.

Smoke cleared to reveal pieces of the door strewn along the hallway inside and a chunk hanging drunkenly from the hinge still. The shilt all wore incredulous faces. 'What?' I asked, 'We're in. Let's get the target and go.'

They were used to being stealthy which was precisely why I was making so much noise. That and because I wanted to wake the people inside. Three of the shilt went ahead of me, the spokesman and two others waiting for me to go in before following.

Lights were already coming on upstairs as I passed over the threshold and into the house. They shone down the stairs until someone on the floor above switched our light on too. Now bathed in bright light, I had to blink as my pupils contracted but I was ready to do what needed to be done.

A man was charging down the stairs. Unfortunately, in this situation, he was the one I was here for. I hadn't been able to tell until now, but with my second sight employed, his aura was clear. The shilt ahead of me were moving in to subdue him but his enraged roar, undoubtedly fuelled by fear, gave me what I needed: An excuse.

I yelled, 'Look out!' as he appeared on the stairs ahead of us. He had a golf club in his hands and wore nothing but a pair of shorts. Yet he represented danger and I had to stop him. At least that was the pretence I employed along with a half-hearted warning cry right before sending a lightning bolt down the hallway.

I acted as if I were trying to save the shilt from harm by targeting the man. I have enough control to create an arc of lightning that will only tickle, right up to one that will fry your insides. It was the latter I conjured, missing the man to *accidentally* spear two of the shilt.

Oops.

Through a terrible twist of fate, it struck their heads and exploded them. As their skulls blew apart from the sudden force inside, I grasped my face and looked horrified.

Above the man on the landing, a woman screamed in terror. The man's own shriek of fright almost drowned hers out until I cut off his oxygen. Killing two of my chaperones was entirely deliberate even if I managed to make it look convincingly like an accident. Their bodies slumped onto one another at the foot of the stairs as the man began to gag.

The remaining shilt, the spokesman especially, growled in rage. 'You killed them on purpose,' their leader accused.

'It was an accident. I thought he might hurt one of them with that club. My aim was off. Lightning is not that easy to control, you know.'

'Then you should not have employed it.'

I nodded my head. 'Yes. We will open the portal directly inside the house next time. This would have been avoided had we done so.'

The shilt showed me its teeth. I felt sure it wanted to threaten me, but what could it threaten me with? Refuse to work with me? Big deal. I don't want to kidnap people anyway and Daniel would blame them not me. If it attacked me, I would kill it and all its brethren. So it showed me its teeth and growled to its colleagues, 'Get the familiar.'

Unable to breathe, the man was on his knees and clutching at his throat. His wife or girlfriend, somehow overcoming her own fear, was rushing to his aid. But the shilt grabbed him before she could, and with his limp form hanging between them, dragged him away. Sensing the shilt was about to open a portal, I placed my hand on its shoulder to give me the skin to skin contact required for crossing and leaned in close to whisper, 'It really was an accident.'

Quietly he growled back, 'I don't believe you.' Then he murmured the incantation, the portal opened behind him and we stepped through.

Chapter 22

The poor man was barely conscious when we stepped into the cool air of the warehouse. I was back again, but this time I wasn't alone with a terrified woman the way I had been the first night. Not that this was any better from the victim's perspective, but I had Gwyneth and Tiberius waiting for me and that was going to make a difference.

We came through the portal on ground level with the smooth concrete beneath my feet. Above us the lights were blazing, making me blink again as my eyes adjusted. The shilt holding the man threw him to the floor as if he disgusted them. He fell to his knees babbling in French.

My French was never good at school, and much worse now fifteen years had passed since my last lesson. I didn't bother trying. Choosing a more universal language instead, I bent down to get into his eyeline, 'It's going to be okay,' I told him in English. 'Can you understand me?'

Looking up from his huddled position on the cold ground, he said, 'Yes.' His eyes betrayed the terror he felt. I had a plan to get him back to his house in a week, but I couldn't tell him about it with four shilt hovering behind me.

Gwyneth and Tiberius were waiting a few metres away until I beckoned them forward. 'This is Tiberius and Gwyneth. They will help you. Listen to them and please try to stay calm.' As his gaze swung to look at the two people approaching, I stepped back and away. I could do nothing for him now and the shilt were waiting.

Joining them, I said, 'Let's go.' Their spokesperson asked, 'Who are they?' pointing to my new companions.

'I recruited them to assist me.' I got a questioning look in response, so I dazzled it with words. 'I questioned a focus group from the last group of new familiars. They felt the experience could be improved in a number of ways. One improvement I have already instigated is the inclusion of a welcoming team. By listening to the feedback we get from each new group, we can really drive some efficiencies in the process, make it slick and ensure we improve our service with each new delivery.'

The shilt don't have eyebrows, but if they did, it's would have been reaching for the hairline it also doesn't have. 'Improve our service?' it repeated slowly, the words dripping out of its mouth as if they tasted foul. 'We are taking humans to be slaves to the demons.'

'Yes,' I replied with a smile. 'But that doesn't mean we cannot enjoy our work and try to do it to the best of our ability.' I paraphrased a superior I tolerated briefly during a job in my early twenties. He was an idiot with no ability or common sense yet somehow still in charge. Who knew the nonsense he spouted back then would come in handy one day? 'Where to next?'

I leaned in close to listen, pretending to check behind me when he said the incantation again. The portal opened, this time when I looked through it, we were clearly inside, but it wasn't a house, it was a shack. We were in a slum.

The portal popped closed behind me as my eyes adjusted yet again to the change in light level. The bright light which shone through the portal from the warehouse briefly had illuminated the inside of the shack and woken the inhabitants. There were at least ten, maybe a dozen, maybe more, and they were all beginning to wake and wail at the strange intruders standing among them.

Over half the people in the tiny shack were children. The shack itself was made of rusting corrugated iron, asbestos sheets and road signs. It was warm inside, the air feeling moist as if I were in a sauna. Then there were two sets of adults I could see, parents to the children and then, grandparents too plus a fifth adult who might be a brother to the children's father. The softly glowing aura came from the grandmother. She had to be nearly seventy.

When the shilt next to me moved, I jabbed out an arm to stop him. 'We leave this one here. She is too old to bother with.' I made it sound like we would be doing ourselves and Daniel a favour.

'That is not the order from Daniel,' the spokesperson argued.

I pulled ley line energy through the ground. 'It is now. Taking her would be a waste of time.' The family were beginning to get up. I was already having to raise my voice to be heard as the adults shouted and the children wailed for their mummy.

Their spokesman made a decision, possibly born of hunger, but foolish either way. 'If we are not to take her, then we will feed.' It was already moving by the time it finished speaking, its brethren fanning out to get to the targets clustered inside the single room dwelling.

Snarling, I snagged a collar and threw that shilt behind me to crash into a wall with a clatter. Then I fired a pulse of air just as one shilt passed in front of the shack's door. The door was secured on the inside by use of a wooden bar which broke in two when the shilt flew through it. Less spectacular than the house in France, the effect was still to leave the dwelling without a front door. I followed that up with a jet of flame to torch the shilt as it rolled in the mud outside. It was dead for sure, but killing it took too long.

The shilts' attention was off the family and firmly on me, which was what I wanted, but killing the first one gave them time to draw their weapons I discovered as one skewered me. I gasped in pain as its obsidian blade went through my abdomen, starting by my right kidney and coming out to the side of my belly button. The pain was excruciating but got worse when I twisted my body to tear the blade from its grasp.

The family were screaming, which was drawing the attention of other people, shouts sounded through the thin walls and through the gaping hole where the door used to be as neighbours awoke and came to investigate. The family were huddled in a corner, children's eyes shielded by their parents and grandparents who could only watch in horror, their only avenue of escape blocked by a wizard kebab and a burning shilt.

FAMILIAR TERRITORY

The remaining three shilt would escape through a portal if I hesitated for a second but I couldn't use lightning or fire in the confined space without hurting or killing the family and I couldn't use an air spell without blowing the shack apart.

That left water and earth and I knew what I had to do. The spokesperson, identifiable from the others only by its clothing, was moving its left hand. He was going to open a portal any second, but it ceased doing anything when I took control of the moisture in its body.

It wasn't easy doing the same spell on three creatures simultaneously, the effort made beads of perspiration pop out on my forehead, though that might have been the strain it took to ignore the pain in my gut. Sticky blood leaked down my belly and my back, soaking my trousers. I felt sick and faint at the same time, but I couldn't let up now.

All three shilt were held in position, unable to resist or fight back as I pushed heat into their cells. The first time I ever tried this, was only two weeks ago and on one of the first occasions I ever fought the shilt. I knew it would work this time; I was just sorry to do it in this poor family's house.

Just before the critical point, I dropped the spell from the meekest of the shilt and pushed yet more energy into the other two. Knowing I had reached the moment, I turned my face away and closed my eyes.

Both shilt exploded from within like a watermelon with a firecracker stuffed inside it. I will admit: it is disgusting. The family, the inside of their shack including the ceiling, two men who had been coming through the open door behind me and, of course, me, were all covered by the exploded gloop that used to be two shilt. It smelled as terrible as it looked which presented one problem because I needed to get clean, but another, far bigger problem, because this would take some explaining when Daniel found out. I didn't have the time to waste on such trivial concerns right now: the last remaining shilt was recovering.

Suddenly dizzy, I could barely keep myself upright. Correction, I couldn't keep myself upright. My knees buckled as my head swam. I was losing a lot of blood, but I could not afford to pass out here. I fell forward, using my left arm to stop the sword poking from my belly from touching the ground.

The remaining shilt was moving, groggily pushing himself upright. With a final lunge, I grabbed his left hand, content he couldn't escape and pushed his fingers open to form the shape they made each time they opened a portal. Then, I repeated the incantation.

'Entour en say na.'

Chapter 23

The portal opened instantly but we were lying on the ground so as it opened behind him, we fell downward through it. This was one element I hadn't considered - how to control where we went.

The portal linked two points, I understood that much, and it did so because the ley lines were connected. Quite why human flesh was wrong for it, I didn't know, but I had proved one thing to myself: I could open a portal if I said the incantation.

The joy of that realisation was very short lived because I arrived in the immortal realm and fell a metre to the ground where the tip of the sword struck the ground first. The searing pain from it made me lose consciousness and vomit, not in that order thankfully.

I awoke a few seconds later in a panic thinking the shilt I came through with must have escaped and by now Daniel would know what I had done. I needed my demon master blind to my activities though I was going to struggle to cover up the murder of five shilt. My rising concern died the moment I looked down to see the shilt beneath me. We tumbled as we fell through the portal and the sword had skewered him to the ground as I fell onto him.

'This is going to hurt, Otto,' I said out loud to gear myself up. I really didn't want to do it, but no one was coming to my rescue, so I closed my mouth to avoid biting my tongue and threw myself backwards. The sword came free of the shilt as I whimpered pathetically from the pain. Now on my knees, I still had to get it out of my back which was an even harder manoeuvre.

I checked the shilt was dead, which it was. I didn't need it waking up and escaping now. Then I reached behind slowly, doing everything I could to not disturb the damned sword prematurely. On a three count which only got to two as I tried to surprise myself, I gripped the blade with both hands and pulled it free. They say size doesn't matter but I screamed every centimetre of that blade and when it was finally free, I let it drop from my right hand and lowered myself carefully back to the ground.

I needed to rest.

The portal had opened in a clearing in a wood. There were stars above me with clouds moving across them and trees all around. Unable to ascertain how the shilt move from A to B in such a way that they know exactly where B is, I ended up wherever the portal took me. Shortly, when the wound had healed, and I felt up to it. I was going to try to cross by myself. I might have the whole thing completely wrong. But maybe I didn't. Maybe I had worked out a way to do this, but crossing was only half the task. I needed to be able to control where I went.

When my eyes began to feel heavy and sleep threatened to take me, I forced myself to start moving. I wasn't ready, the taste of bile sat thick in my mouth making me want to retch again. I had work to do; I focussed on that.

Thankful for the shilt's sword, I cut its left hand off and did something I never imagined I would: I made a glove from its skin. If that sounds like a disgusting thing to do, let me assure it was far worse than I am making it sound. It wasn't fast either; I didn't want to risk hurrying and ripping the flesh. Would a torn glove work? I had no idea if it would work anyway, but keeping it intact had to be better, right? It was sticky with blood and desperately horrible to put on, but after maybe an hour of careful work, I had the hand from another creature encasing my own.

Now for the moment of truth.

I sniffed in a deep breath to steady myself, feeling nervous that this might be a huge disappointment. Splaying my fingers the same way the shilt did, I murmured, 'Entour en say na,' and pictured a place I wanted very much to go.

My assumption was that the shilt, demon, or whatever creature was crossing between realms, was able to determine their destination by visualising it in their head. They travelled because of the ley line connection, the lines criss-crossing the planet to reach almost every point. I imagined the lines, seeing them in my head as I visualised the journey from where I was to where I wanted to be. The portal opened and when I ducked my head and stepped through it, I let go the breath I held and felt the tension in my shoulders ease.

Then I did a little dance on the spot and punched my right hand into the air. If legends were true, I was the first ever human to travel between realms. The first to figure it out and all I had done was employ a lesson I learned from the werewolf. He saw the practical solution to problems - the simple solution.

When the shilt told me human skin couldn't open a portal, I instantly asked myself what might happen if I clothed myself in different skin. Now thankful all it took was a glove, not a full body suit, because that would be truly repulsive, I had done it.

I've got to tell you, I felt magnificent.

I knew it was a touch too early to celebrate yet, so I shoved my excitement back down and jogged across the snow to the house I chose to picture in my head. It wasn't mine; there was nothing I needed there, it was the house of Heike Dressler and she was going to prove very useful.

I didn't know what time it was, but it didn't matter. It was way after bedtime, and she wouldn't be happy to be disturbed since I would have to wake the whole house. Despite that, the clock was ticking so I was going to do it anyway.

My loud thumping resulted in a light appearing inside the house a few seconds later. It was followed by an argument, a woman and a man both raising their voices until the man accepted he was going to get his butt kicked if he persisted. Then, the light just inside the door went on and one just above my head a second before the door opened a crack.

The eyeball peering out at me through the sliver of open door registered surprise and finally the door opened to reveal Heike wearing a coat and very little else. Actually, she might be fully dressed beneath it, but all I could see was the coat.

'Otto? What the hell are you doing here? What the hell happened to you. Get inside quickly.'

I didn't need to be told twice; I was already moving when she spoke. Time was of paramount importance. Babbling to get my words out, I blurted, 'My apologies for the timing of my visit. I have a few things to explain but I really need your help.'

The door closed behind me and I turned to find Heike leaning on it. 'I have a warrant for your arrest,' she announced. She didn't look happy about it and wasn't pointing a gun at me, so I didn't think she was telling me I needed to get on my knees and be ready for the cuffs. 'You really do have some explaining to do.'

'Any chance of a coffee?' I asked, the idea suddenly occurring to me.

She pushed off the door but then noticed the footprint I left on her carpet. 'Oh, my God, is that blood?' she asked, her eyes bugging out at the fresh red making her blue carpet purple.

Guiltily, I hopped back onto the mat just inside her door making an oops face. In my haste and excitement, I forgot I was covered in shilt goo and my own blood which had soaked my lower half. Most of the shilt innards had already sloughed off, dripped off, or otherwise left me, but a quick glance in her hall mirror showed me how ghastly I looked.

Seeing my apologetic smile, she frowned at me. 'Strip.'

'Beg pardon?'

'Strip. Come on, wizard. I'm not letting you in my house looking like that and you are going to help me clean that gunk out of my carpet. So strip. This is just like the time you exploded a pair of shilt in the morgue.' She gasped. 'Is that what that is? Do I have shilt guts in my carpet?' Now I had her angry face and a deep frown.

Carefully, I opened my coat to show her the tear in my shirt which I untucked to reveal the wound on my stomach. It had closed and healed over but the skin was pink where the new flesh had formed and would not return to normal for at least an hour. 'I got skewered,' I told her. 'Most of that is my blood, sorry. I'm sure that isn't much better.'

She pursed her lips and nodded. 'I'll get a sack for your clothes. Let's get you fixed up and clean. Then we'll talk.' Leaving me on the doormat to go in search of what she needed, she called back over her shoulder, 'Strip, wizard. Or do you need me to play some dance music?'

Twenty minutes later I was sitting at her kitchen table with a sandwich and a hot cup of coffee. I was dressed in some of Franz's clothes just like I had last time this happened. I failed to return the last outfit he surrendered, yet I wasn't given rubbishy old hand-me-downs; I had a lined winter rain coat which fell to midway down my thighs, a black shirt with a thin charcoal sweater and a pair of dark grey hopsack trousers. They were a touch short in the leg, but most of the items looked nearly new. If giving up his wardrobe bothered him, I was certain Heike made the selection, Franz knew well enough to not comment.

'Do you know anything about Katja Weber?' I asked. 'She wanted me to train her.' In truth I was worried for how her father might treat her now he knew she was different. I felt that she needed someone, not necessarily me, but someone, who could help and guide her.

Heike pulled a grim face. 'I think she has been training herself.' Knowing her statement would require some expansion, she added, 'She has been in trouble with the police twice this week that I know of. She started a fire at the mall. She denied it but a score of witnesses said she used a flamethrower.' I gawked in my surprise, not at the story itself but that she was able to produce fire. It took me years to learn that skill. 'They had to let her go because, of course, she didn't have a flamethrower. The police got called to her school as well when two girls got hurt. No one would talk about it. Especially not the two girls, but I was one of the officers attending and could see they wouldn't look at her.'

'How were they hurt? In what way?' I asked.

'Just bruising. It happened during soccer practice. Again, I had to go off witness statements.'

'I thought you said no one would talk.'

'None of the girls would. It was the teachers who told me both girls flew into the air and then fell back to the ground. They both said they reached a height of at least four metres. They were lucky to get away with bruising.'

I nodded. They were lucky. Katja revealed she got bullied. I guess she had enough and snapped.

Awake with all the activity in his house, Franz came to join us for coffee. He interrupted our discussion just as I was switching it from the less important subject of Katja to the far more pertinent one of where I had been and what I was doing to remedy my situation. Heike saw her husband's inclusion as a good time to make an announcement.

'Just like that?' Franz asked. 'Without discussing it with me first?'

Heike gave him a raised eyebrow. 'What is there to discuss, Franz? You never liked that I was in the police anyway, now I am not.'

He shook his head in irritation. 'I wanted you to leave the police because we didn't need the money and the kids wanted you at home. Now you tell me you have joined some supernatural investigation team.'

'Alliance,' she corrected him.

'Whatever,' he growled. 'It doesn't sound any safer, Heike. Why would you do that?'

'Because of what is coming, Franz. They need more people.'

He screwed his face up. 'Because of what is coming? What does that mean? What is coming?'

She turned her face to look directly at me. 'Tell him, Otto.'

I was already feeling quite uncomfortable. I was in someone else's house wearing someone else's clothes and now I was privy to a spousal argument. What I wanted to do was slink away until they were finished, not bring myself into the middle of it. Heike's expression wasn't going to let me off the hook any time soon, so I started talking. 'An army of demons is going to invade the Earth and take control of the planet, wiping out a good portion of humanity as they do it.'

Franz stared at me for a second then his face fought for the right expression. Flitting between mirth because I had to be joking, and then concern when neither Heike nor I smiled, he finally settled on fear that I might be telling the truth.

He asked a question. 'Why did she call you a wizard?'

I drew on a ley line and made a flame in my hand. Franz jumped backward off his chair and darted across the room never once taking his eyes off me. Since I had an audience, I doused the flame and caused his coffee to swirl in its cup, turning it into a waterspout that funnelled upward half a metre in a tall tube. As I let it go, the liquid, probably now cool, splashed back into his cup with a plop, I then froze it and said. Locking eyes, I said, 'Because I am a wizard.'

For good measure, I took out the shilt glove, a terrible piece of scaly leather with fleshy bits still hanging off it. 'This is the skin of a creature the demons use as foot soldiers. They feed on the life energy inside people and were responsible for a spate of deaths a couple of weeks back.'

'And since,' said Heike. 'There have been more in the week since you vanished. What happened at the dockyard? Reports were sketchy but they found the charred remains of Zuzana Brychta and from the descriptions, it sounded like you were fighting Daniel when the cops arrived.'

'That's what happened. I fought him but there were some parts of the bargain I didn't understand and his binding of me is absolute. He can control my body. Through the binding he can render me completely unable to move or make me use my own body to defend him.'

'Is that why you have been kidnapping people?' Heike asked, her husband's jaw dropping open at the question.

'Yes,' I replied. 'Is that why you have a warrant for my arrest?' Franz threw his arms in the air in disbelief.

'They caught you on camera. You were with Daniel in most of the shots I saw. One of the women you took is the daughter of an American politician. Ayla Pendragon?'

The information didn't surprise me, but it also didn't change anything. I downed the rest of my coffee and stood up. 'Thank you for your hospitality, Heike and for your clothes, Franz. This is the second time you have emptied your wardrobe for me. I need to go, but I expect to be back soon. A couple of days maybe and I will be bringing as many people with me as possible.'

'People?' Franz and Heike both asked together.

I took a few minutes to explain what I was doing and what I now hoped to achieve. 'I need you to get the Alliance organised to receive them. They need to come into a holding facility and be looked after while we reintegrate them.'

'Why can't we just send them home?' asked Franz. It was a valid question.

'Some of them have been trapped in the immortal realm for decades. Others have been there for more than a century. This world will be very disorientating for them so I will need somewhere secure to put them. People like Ayla Pendragon can go home but imagine going back to New York if you last saw it in the 1800s. What if you were taken fifteen years ago? Your husband or wife is still alive but now married to someone else and your kids have grown up and don't know you. If we don't control them, some will implode.' They both saw the truth of it. There would be elements I hadn't considered, which was why I needed Heike to start pulling strings. I hadn't known she was switching sides to be a part of the Alliance; the team trying to keep this from the global population and work out a way to stop it happening, but it probably helped that she was.

Heike only asked one question, 'How soon?'

'As soon as I can. A few days I expect.'

Staying here to coordinate it myself would be nice but also impractical. I had to get back to the warehouse, plus I still needed to work out how to cover up the death of my shilt escort, my sudden ability to move between the realms by myself, and explain to Daniel why I only took one new familiar when he expected five.

Choosing to show off, I slipped the shilt glove back onto my left hand. Heike and Franz both watched me with questioning looks, wondering what trick I might be about to employ. Standing in their kitchen, I murmured the incantation and opened a portal to the warehouse in the immortal realm. A quick glance over my shoulder told me I had successfully created the bridge between two points. Determining where I wanted to go and making it happen was surprisingly easy. Then, with a waggle of my eyebrows at their shocked faces, I left them behind and stepped back into the immortal realm.

My stupid confidence set a tripwire that I alone triggered.

My timing could not have been worse.

Chapter 24

The poor Frenchman, whose name I had yet to learn, was kneeling on the floor before Daniel. What was he doing here? My heart caught in my throat as the portal closed behind me. It was too late for me to open another and escape, Daniel was already turning around. Where were Tiberius and Gwyneth? Had he already caught them? Karen and Rita were standing off to one side. They had brought clothing I could see; a pile of it left on the floor by their feet.

I thrust my left hand into my pocket and gave the demon a weary smile, waving with my right hand and trying to look casual as I approached.

'Why is he the only one?' Daniel demanded.

I blew out a breath of frustration. 'The night was a total bust. We got this one without any bother, but the next one was an old Indian lady in terrible health who had a heart attack the moment we got there. Then, when the shilt took me to the next two places, the targets weren't there.'

'Weren't there?'

'Yes. As in, they were not there. No trace of a magical aura to be found. How old is your information? I know you get it from the shilt but one place they took me to was a motel. Do they understand that the people staying there are transient?' I was lying through my teeth now I had a flow going.

Daniel looked about. 'Where are they?'

'The shilt?' Ha! Try getting them to deny what I am telling you. 'I had them open a portal so I could return and left them behind on Earth. They said they had to feed. Actually, they spent most of the night complaining that they needed to feed but I wouldn't let them. I refused to watch, but they are back there now somewhere sucking the life out of some poor soul no doubt.' My mouth was running away now. I was never this chatty. I clammed up and mentally folded my top lip over my bottom one.

Daniel did not look entirely convinced but did not elect to call me a liar. 'Very well, Otto. Do what you can with this one, but I expect better results on the morrow. Beelzebub has charged me with providing more familiars. It is not in your interest to let me down.'

As he walked away, Karen and Rita following silently behind, I held my breath. Letting it go with sigh of relief when the door closed. My heart had been thudding in my chest since I crossed through the portal and found him here. I felt sure all my plans were going up in smoke. A noise to my right made me start. Automatically I drew ley line energy into my body as I slipped the glove off to leave it in my pocket. Two heads peered around the corner of a steel column.

Gwyneth and Tiberius gave me a nervous grin. 'Is he gone?' mouthed Gwyneth with a loud whisper.

'Yes. I think so. How did you get on? In fact, how did you manage to hide?'

Tiberius answered. 'We always thought there was a danger he might show up here, so we were partially hidden from the door throughout. Did you really send the shilt back to feed?'

'Of course not. They're all dead.' I turned my attention to the Frenchman. 'How is he?'

Tiberius called to him, his voice soft and caring. 'Raymond.' The man lifted his head. 'Raymond the demon has gone. You are safe now.' Raymond did not look convinced that he could trust the verdict of safety and who could blame him?

I went to him, offering my hand to help him up. 'Raymond, I am sorry for what has happened to you. Please believe me when I claim that I would have avoided taking you if I could have.'

His eyes flicked to Tiberius and Gwyneth. 'They say you are trying to help me.'

'You probably find that hard to believe right now, but it is true. Were it not me that took you from your home, it would have been someone else. I cannot predict how long you might be here, but I will stress that you need to embrace your magical side, it may yet save your life.' Over my shoulder I asked the others, 'Does he have any skill?'

'Some,' replied Tiberius chewing a nail. 'He discovered he could heat water but didn't understand how he was doing it. From there he developed a set of skills to control and manipulate water. He works as an ice sculptor.'

As my face formed a question, Raymond began to look embarrassed. 'I do it in private,' he admitted. 'I don't let anyone come into my studio ever so they cannot see how I do it.' Then to demonstrate, he drew ley line energy through his body and used it to coalesce water in his palm. There was no water in the room, so he took it from the air, and as it gathered into a small orb above his right palm, he formed it into a shape and froze it. In his hand was a perfectly formed, tiny horse made from ice.

'That is quite something,' I complimented his work. 'It is also how they found you. You drew quite a bit of magical energy to complete that spell. Tiberius and Gwyneth will show you how to better understand it and use it in different ways.'

Tiberius said, 'We will have to get back to our master's soon.'

'We have been here all night,' added Gwyneth.

It was important that no one drew unnecessary attention. The last thing we wanted was the demons dropping their complacent attitude. We were going to escape and confound them because they were so utterly confident we could do neither thing. I had the glove and could open a portal but chose to keep that my secret for now. My decision wasn't to make myself seem mystical and brilliant. Rather, I wasn't sure what I could do with it yet – more testing was required before I could claim I had our route home worked out.

I stayed for an hour to teach Raymond how to manipulate air, calling it to him and pushing it away. I wanted to distract him as much as possible because he would be alone for the rest of the day. I was going to get him home, and he just had to hold on to that belief until I delivered.

'I just have to wait here?' he asked.

I placed a hand on his shoulder, attempting to impart strength and confidence. 'For now. Until I can return you home, you are better off staying here in this warehouse. I fear I may have to bring others to join you tonight. The best thing you can do is practice what we have taught you and keep your strength up. Eat what Karen and Rita bring you. Sleep when you can and practice the spells. I intend for us to slip away unnoticed, but that might not come to pass, and we should be ready to fight.'

I think my last comment scared him more than anything else. I didn't feel bad about it, only bad that he had to be here in the first place.

Leaving the building, the shilt guarding it eyeing me warily yet again, a shadow detached itself from the wall to step out into the sunlight. For a moment, I thought it was Tiberius and wondered why he hadn't hurried home as he claimed he needed to do. However, I saw instantly that I was mistaken, it was Sean McGuire, the Irish Wizard.

'Good morning, Otto,' he called jovially as if we were old friends. I had no reason to expect him to seek me out, yet here he was and being friendly. Yesterday I asked him about whether he ever thought about escaping. Now he was looking for me.

Seeing no reason not to return his pleasantry, I replied, 'Good morning, Sean. What brings you here?'

'You do.' When I cocked an eyebrow at him, he chuckled because he knew he was being cryptic. 'I thought about what you were saying last night, and I think you might be onto something.'

There was nothing veiled within his words; no lie making itself known, but his shift in attitude confused me. 'I thought you said the demons couldn't be beaten no matter what and that they would just track down a familiar if they ever did work out how to escape back to Earth.'

He didn't argue. 'I did say that, yes. I might have been a bit hasty, though. I think maybe I have just been here so long under the demons' cosh, so to speak, that the idea of anything else threw me for a bit of a loop.'

'I see. What are you saying? You think it might be possible to evade the demons if we were able to return to Earth?'

Sean shrugged; an exaggerated move that brought his shoulders up next to his ears. 'I'm not sure I would go that far, but I would be willing to explore the opportunity if there were like-minded individuals to discuss such a thing with.'

'The demons will see it as treachery if they catch us,' I warned him, testing to see how easily he could be put off.

'That they might,' he agreed. 'They might even kill a few of us if we were caught. Most likely they would force us to fight, familiar against familiar, that is their tradition. It entertains them to see us fight to the death.'

'You have some experience in that, I hear.' I was pushing him to see where his boundaries might lie. I got the impression Byron and the others didn't trust him, but that didn't mean he couldn't be trusted, only that he had chosen, with limited options, to feather his nest and make the best of it.

He looked disappointed when he replied. 'You are not wrong, I'm afraid. It was never something I wanted, but Nathaniel, my master, once he realised I was strong enough to win against other familiars, he began goading his rival demons. Beelzebub didn't approve but Nathaniel is cruel and malicious and would challenge him for the right to rule if he thought he could win.'

Sean was revealing inside knowledge, and again I could tell he was being truthful. Was it a deliberate ploy to gain my trust? 'If he is so cruel, why were you so swift to use your body to prevent my attack scoring a hit the other day?'

A small snort of laughter escaped him. 'Because he expects it of me and had you tagged him with that lightning strike, he would have taken it out on me later. His punishment would be far worse than anything you could dish out.'

It wasn't intended as an insult and I took no offense from it. I needed to get back to Daniel's house and rest, I was scoring very little sleep because of my dual life working for Daniel and trying to organise a revolt. Starting back in that direction, I invited Sean to walk with me.

'Do you have any kind of plan, Otto?' he asked.

'For escape? I have parts of a plan. As you so rightly pointed out; if we cannot break the binding, there is no point attempting to leave. That is our biggest hurdle. Anyone who could provide a clue as to how we achieve that would be our greatest champion.'

'Aye, it's a tough one,' Sean agreed. 'Do you not think it might be an insurmountable challenge?'

I had to smile at his question. 'If I thought that, I never would have started to question how to escape. If we assume a thing isn't possible, then we ourselves make it impossible. Our minds become the barrier to success. Who says it cannot be done? The demons? Of course they do; they don't want us to even try to free ourselves. Imagine the power they lose if we can undo the binding they place upon us.'

Sean paused, falling behind me as I took another pace. 'I am going this way, Otto,' he pointed through the woods. 'You have given me much to think about and I will seek you out again soon. Tell me, are there many who you feel will join you?'

'A few for sure, but I do not know how many and I do not know who I can trust.'

'Aye, 'tis a hard thing to talk about openly, given the potential ramifications if our masters learn of it.' He smiled just before he turned, his path taking him between some trees to vanish moments later between the denuded winter foliage.

Sean McGuire: could I trust him or not?

Chapter 25

I was by myself for the first time in days I realised as I continued onward to Daniel's house. Okay, technically I was by myself a few hours ago when I came through the portal to land on top of the shilt. He was dead at that point but given the state I was in, it wasn't as if I could have done anything constructive with the lack of chaperones.

Partly because I had the means of travel, partly because I was brimming with excitement to continue trying out the portal, but also out of concern because Heike told me she was in trouble, I chose to find Katja. I looked all around, checking to see if there was anyone who might spot me, and content there was not, I slipped my hand inside my pocket to get the glove.

I felt decidedly ill at ease as I opened a portal into the bedroom of a fifteen-year-old girl, but I did so with the best intentions. I couldn't keep up with what day it was, despite trying to work it out in my head. At best guess it was a Wednesday or a Thursday, but even if it were a Saturday, I expected her bedroom to be empty at this time of the day. Assuming time zones worked the same in the immortal realm; it was under the same sun after all, then it was mid-morning and she would be at school or out with her friends.

Just in case she was, in fact, home and in a state of undress, I closed my eyes when I opened the portal. 'Katja?' I asked tentatively.

When I got no answer, I risked a peek. I was still standing in the immortal realm, looking through it into a bedroom I recognised from two previous visits to the house; once when Daniel took her and once when I returned to fight Teague.

FAMILIAR TERRITORY

Thinking of Teague reminded me of Ayla and her plight, my top lip twitching in anger once again until I banished the errant train of thought. Katja clearly wasn't in her room, so I stepped through the portal and let it close behind me. There was no sound in the house when I paused to listen for a minute, but even though I could take my time, the sensible choice was to get the task done and get out quickly.

Finding a notebook on her bedside table, I snapped it up. A pen with a fluffy unicorn topper poked from an elastic loop. It wrote the same as a normal pen, thankfully – no sparkles or glitter leaking from it as I scrawled her a note. I tore out the page, folded it and tucked it into her pillow where I was certain she would find it. The task complete, I opened a portal back to where I had been and stepped from her bedroom to the path by the woods on the way back to Daniel's house.

'Otto!' Hearing my name being called startled me, making me spin about to face the direction it came from.

Emerging from the trees behind me were Meilin and Chen, Bryon's friends. They almost caught me with the portal open, not that it would necessarily matter if they did, but I wanted to keep it my secret for now. If this all fell apart, if the demons found out, I might need a means of escape no one else knew about.

The two Chinese women were approaching with long strides over the rough grass that led from the woods to the path I was on. I waited for them with a smile until they were within earshot at normal speaking volume.

'We saw Gwyneth this morning,' Chen announced. 'She said you were able to limit the number of familiars you brought through last night and that you killed the shilt that escorted you.'

'Yes, that's correct. I doubt I will be able to pull the same trick twice and I worry the missing shilt will raise a question later.'

Chen seemed less concerned. 'I carry a message from Byron.' When my eyebrows raised, she proceeded. 'He wasn't sure if he could trust you which is why Tiberius and Gwyneth agreed to assist you last night. Their report confirms that you are as you claim to be.'

Their doubt should not be a surprise to me, yet it was. I felt I won them over the previous afternoon and now discovered Tiberius and Gwyneth only agreed to help so they could spy on me. 'You feel you can trust me now?'

'The sudden appearance of a new wizard with surprising powers and claims of immortality is shocking enough, yet you then revealed a plan for escape. It made us very suspicious. The desire to escape is not a new one but any hint of rebellion against our masters in the past has been met with severe repercussions. No one has talked of such a thing in many years. However, Byron believes you are what you say and that is good enough for us.'

'I have part of a plan. I feel confident I can get us all back to Earth.'

'By forcing a shilt to open a portal?' asked Meilin.

I shook my head. 'No. When the time comes, I will open the portal myself.' It was a bold statement and got the looks it deserved.

Meilin challenged me, 'How will you do that?'

Remembering a line from a film, I smiled when I said, 'A magician never reveals his secrets. Just trust me on this.' I sure hoped I was right now my big mouth had made the boast. It wasn't like I had thoroughly tested my new ability yet. Maybe the glove would stop working. Maybe I wouldn't be able to take people through with me. Telling myself they were concerns for another time, I pressed on. 'We still need to work on the binding. In order to decode it, we need to understand how it works. They use a drop of our blood to form the initial binding but after that they can transfer it to another demon at will. Do they need another drop of blood? How is the transfer achieved? If we know those things, maybe we can change our future and strike back against them.'

'We are working on it,' Meilin promised. 'We bring you other news. There are more of us.'

'You mean more that are ready to risk their lives for the chance of escape?'

'Yes,' she replied.

FAMILIAR TERRITORY

I wasn't sure how to feel about this. My brag about Spartacus made me feel heroic at the time. It was a grand plan, a fantastic plan. In some ways, having a small army of familiars join my cause was attractive. There would be strength in numbers, yet the wider we cast our circle of inclusion, the more likely discovery became.

When I voiced my concern, certain it wasn't the first time I had done so, Chen did her best to reassure me. 'You are a new arrival, but of course many have been here for decades or even centuries like Byron. We have learned to communicate in secret, and we know who we can and cannot trust. When we sent a coded note out last night to ask who would rally, the response was better than we expected. There is need for caution, but we have friends who we will take with us if we are able to go.'

Accepting what she told me and hoping it was true, I sucked air between my teeth and said, 'We need to meet. If we are to break our binding, we must all work together.'

'Come with us, Otto. There is much to discuss,' Meilin pressed.

'With Byron?'

'And others,' said Chen. 'We will only get one shot at doing this. Our planning must not only be completely invisible to the demons, it must also include as many of us as is possible. These two desires are counter-intuitive, trying to do one makes the other so much harder. However, Byron will not agree, and others will not follow unless we are to try to get all who wish to escape.

In the space of a day, my plan to break my binding and escape with a few familiars had grown arms and legs. This was a full jail break now, as many familiars as possible. Just how many did that mean?

I guessed finding out might have to take a backseat when Carenis stepped onto the path through the woods to block our route.

Chapter 26

Nathaniel thought about his familiar's unexpected revelation. According to Sean, Daniel's new familiar wasn't just looking to escape, he was organising a rebellion. It was the sweetest news his ears could possibly receive. Now he just needed to engineer the result a little so he could emerge as the champion who averted it and his journey to put Daniel back in his place would be complete.

Sean would see to it that he aided Otto in bringing together all those familiars who were disloyal. Many times Nathaniel had warned Beelzebub about the practice of gathering so many over such a short space of time. Before the death curse, they never needed to steal humans in the night; the humans would volunteer. It was a service with benefits, for the familiar would be permitted to raise a family and they would be safe from harm against creatures that might prey on them and always well fed. A volunteer was worth ten pressed humans, he reminded their leader more than once.

Nathaniel would swoop to stop their escape at the last moment, saving many demons from the embarrassment of losing their familiar or familiars. It would raise his standing and allow him to carefully question how it was that their leader, Beelzebub, had been so blind to the uprising. The death curse was going to fail and the fight for Earth would come. When it did, he would be able to kill Beelzebub and claim his rightful position at the top of demon society. Between now and then, he needed to cement his position as rightful heir in the minds of the community and this was going to get him a long way towards his goal.

There was work to do now and he had to be swift with it for fear of missing his chance. What Nathaniel didn't understand was how Otto Schneider proposed to escape. He could threaten a shilt, but the shilt would know it was suicide to comply; the demons would kill it the moment they found out, so it was a plan with a low probability of success. No demon would open a portal to let the familiars escape, he was fairly certain of that, but what options did that leave? There were a few other creatures that could open a portal for themselves, but none that wouldn't kill and eat the familiar asking the question. If necessary, he would manufacture a way to escape. There were demons who owed him and some who wanted to gain his favour; maybe he could have one act the role of traitor so the familiars would attempt an escape.

'Yes,' he said out loud. 'Antimia. She has no familiar and has spoken once too often on the subject in public.' Sean waited patiently for his master to explain, well used to the demon voicing his thoughts without desire for response. 'I will instruct her to act as the honey in this trap. The familiars will believe it.' Nathaniel explained his instructions to Sean and made him recite them back to him to show his detailed understanding. Then he was dismissed, the familiar leaving to exact his master's plan while Nathaniel summoned Antimia.

Sean would infiltrate the inner circle; Nathaniel had given him the tools to do that – a way for the familiars to break the binding - and now it was up to his familiar to prove his worth. Antimia had a key role in this and maybe, once Daniel was cast back down to his rightful place under Nathaniel's heel, Nathaniel would grant her the familiar she so vocally desired.

His plan relied upon revealing a piece of ancient demon magic he knew others would consider too sensitive for the familiars to know. He disagreed. They would not be able to break the binding even with the information he gave Sean, but with Antimia playing her role correctly, they would try and that would be enough for Nathaniel to prove what they were trying to do. He would catch them, carry sentence on them, and show that it was he alone who deserved all the credit.

The demons would praise him for his insight while he ruined Daniel and cast doubt on Beelzebub's rule.

It was masterful.

Chapter 27

'What do you want, ogre?' demanded Chen, drawing ley line energy. Meilin did the same which prompted me to do likewise. He didn't seem even slightly intimidated. In fact, he would need to lie down to look more relaxed.

'I will speak with Daniel's familiar,' his deep voice rumbled. His words carried threat of violence yet to be wrought.

Unsure where this was heading and wondering how tough an ogre was, I said, 'I can hear you.'

Carenis bared his teeth and bunched his legs a little as if getting ready to pounce. 'Six shilt left with you last night. None have returned. What became of them?'

Briefly, I thought about telling him a lie and trying to bluff my way out. He didn't look like he cared for what my answer might be, and I was sure he already suspected the truth, so I decided to find out if he was as tough as he looked. He was going to leap the moment he saw me begin to conjure, and I remembered Daniel telling me he could render an effective shield, so I used my air spell to evade his initial attack. He saw my hands move and leapt, exploding forward with a wild snarl. As I pushed the air down to propel myself into the air, the women to my left and right did likewise to put all three of us above his head when he crashed into the space we just occupied.

'We have to stop him!' I yelled. 'If he tells Daniel ...' I didn't need to say anything more, the ramifications were obvious, and they were both already coming back to the ground with spells in their hands.

Screaming in Chinese, Chen launched a salvo of rocks from the earth, each as large as a watermelon. The ogre was spinning about but his massive size made him slow. He caught the first enormous rock with his face and the second a breath later on his chest. The third, though, he punched from the air as if it were a piñata. It exploded into a shower of smaller pieces and dust which clouded his position. Unable to see him for a moment when the fourth rock disappeared into the cloud, Chen failed to anticipate the rock coming back at her.

It flew across the space at twice the speed, hurtling toward her just as the ogre roared and leapt into the clearer air. Now he was mad, a trickle of blood coming from his blocky left eyebrow where the first rock cut him. I threw down lightning, stabbing the earth with forks of it gathered far above my head, but his shield, a curved rectangle more than two metres in each direction, diffused my blasts, grounding them each time as he remained unscathed.

I switched attack, Meilin getting in first as she too pelted him with lightning, but nothing was penetrating.

'Split up!' Chen yelled, seeing the need to divide his attention. 'Hit him from three sides!'

We all tried to move position at the same time, creating yet more confusion which Carenis took advantage of. From his belt, he produced a set of bolas, a weapon I had only ever seen on television. His shield was in his left hand, the weapon in his right and spinning already as he scanned around to select a target. Whatever else they might be, I was certain they were not ordinary bolas which he proved a moment later when he launched them at Meilin.

They made a noise as they ripped through the air. It sounded like a firework rocketing into the sky. Meilin barely got out of the way in time, throwing herself backward and flat to the ground as they tore over her head. Missing their target, they carried on to strike a tree where they exploded, the tree seeming to jump half a metre before crashing back down and toppling to the side.

That wasn't the weapon expended though. Far from it. The ogre held out his hand to receive the still spinning bolas as they returned to it.

Focussing his attention on Meilin made an opening for Chen and me to manoeuvre. We were now behind him to his left and right. With Meilin we formed three points on the circumference of a circle with him in the middle.

If he got one of us with the bolas, it might spell the end for the other two as well; he was holding his own easily against the three of us and it reminded me of what Sean said about the humans not standing a chance against the forces Beelzebub would bring.

I screamed, 'Heat him up!' trying to coordinate our efforts in a way that he wouldn't be able to fight. It was no good trying to use physical weapons because his shield would protect him, but my instruction wasn't clear enough so as I ripped the cells in his body and tried to apply heat, both women threw flame at him.

Meilin's jet of fire hit his shield where any threat from it was instantly extinguished, but Chen's got through, torching his back to extract a roar of pain-fuelled rage. She should have expected the bolas to come her way, but either she didn't, or she just wasn't able to move fast enough because they flew across the space between to wrap around her. I didn't watch as they exploded; I didn't want to see, but when no shout of pain came back, I suspected the worst.

Meilin shrieked in horror, her flame failing as she lost her concentration. The bolas were deadly, and they would fly back to his hand at any moment. My attempts to superheat his body weren't putting him down, but that made my decision to switch tactic easy. As the bolas span back toward their owner, I conjured a simple air spell and plucked them from his grasp with a blast of wind. I was ready for what he might throw at me next, at least I told myself I was, but whatever might come, I put everything into an earth spell that opened a hole and buried the bolas before the ogre could react.

I got an angry roar in response which elicited a grin of defiance from me. Now disarmed, I was going to kill him.

Her face filled with tears, Meilin cried out, 'Earth, Otto. Together!'

I knew she was right. It was the surest way to disable him at this stage and one I would remember if I ever came up against an ogre again. We both pulled yet more energy from the line beneath our feet, channelling our efforts into the ground to grasp a section of ground beneath Carenis's feet. I had never worked with another elemental magic practitioner like this, our spells combining as we worked together. I could feel her spell moving around mine as we dug into the soil. We were going to carve out a huge divot and open it up, dropping the ogre into a giant hole and burying him in it. He couldn't see or feel what we were doing, and now disarmed he couldn't throw anything, but he was going to attack.

'Otto, now!' shouted Meilin, telling me to pull the pin on our spell, but as the ground began to shift, Carenis leapt. It was exactly what I wanted him to do. As he sailed through the air, I dropped all the effort in my previous earth spell and pushed all I could muster into a new one. The ogre came back to Earth, and I got to see the shocked look on his face as he fell straight into the pit I opened. With gravity guiding him, there was no way to avoid the fresh hole in the ground.

The moment he vanished into it, I closed it over again. Trapping him twenty metres below the surface with no air. For good measure I ran to the freshly closed hole and stamped on the dirt to compact it down.

I wanted to feel triumphant, but the soft keening of Meilin drew my attention across the path to where she lay cradling Chen's ruined body.

That Chen was dead could not be questioned. The bolas had struck her midriff and torn her almost in two. Meilin cradled her top half. To say I felt responsible would be an understatement; I created the situation that led to this. Her death made me want to stop, to reconsider all that I planned, but it would mean her death had no reason at all. I had to be stronger now and push through to achieve a goal Chen believed was worth dying for.

However, her death created a new problem I could not ignore. Her master would notice she was missing. The demon might even notice the change in Meilin who would not be able to mask her grief. Carenis too might be missed. For all I knew, he had family, or maybe it would be the shilt who reported his absence. Whatever the case, our timeline just changed to urgent. It was that or delay it for long enough for this to blow over and I wasn't sure that would be possible.

Oddly, as I tried to comfort Meilin and thought about what to do with Chen's body, rescue came in a form I did not expect.

Chapter 28

I caught sight of him in the air because he crossed the sun and cast a shadow. I didn't know who it was, only that someone was flying, and I had only seen wizards or witches do that. They were coming at me out of the sun, making it impossible to make out any detail. For all I knew it was a giant flying monster about to chew me to death.

Preparing for the worst, I tapped into the ley line and got my body in front of Meilin's. If it came to a fight, she would either be too overcome by her emotions to lend a hand, or so fuelled by rage that she would kill without thinking.

I held an air spell in my hand and got ready to throw it, but the sound of Sean's voice stopped me. 'Oh, no. Otto, what happened here?'

I pushed myself off the ground, but kept the spell loaded. Sean would know I was carrying it, or at least, carrying something. He would be able to see the ley line energy running into me and know I was drawing energy to power a conjuring. He wasn't wary, though. The moment he touched down five metres away, he started walking toward me, his eyes on Chen and Meilin more than on me.

'We were attacked by Carenis,' I told him.

'Damned ogres,' Sean spat. 'Virtually indestructible, mean as all hell and the demons have barely any control over them.' He knelt next to Chen's feet where he silently shook his head. He looked sad; genuinely distressed at the sight of her body. 'We must report this. The demons need to react. Acadus will tear Carenis into pieces for lowering his status.'

Quietly I said, 'Carenis is already dead.'

Sean's head snapped around to look up at me. 'You managed to kill him? You're tougher than I thought. How did you manage it?'

'I buried him in the ground.'

Sean looked about and spotted the fresh scar where the soil had recently been turned. Nodding, he said, 'Impressive.' Then, glancing back down at Chen, he added, 'But not without cost.'

Meilin, slowly lowered Chen back to the ground. 'Will you help me?' she asked. 'I want to bury her.'

Of course. Time was a critical factor, but I couldn't ignore Meilin's wish to perform a final ritual for her friend.

It didn't take long. It wasn't as if we had to dig a hole with our hands. Sean combined with me to create a hole in the earth, and we carefully lowered Chen into it. Meilin sang a song in her native tongue, a haunting tune that I couldn't understand.

Neither Sean nor I said a word, but when she was finished, I placed a hand on her shoulder. 'We need to go,'

Sean put a hand out to stop us, 'Otto, I sought you out because I have important news. You should both hear this; it affects us all.'

Curious enough to indulge him, I gave him my full attention. 'Tell me what you have, Sean.'

'It's to do with breaking the binding. You said you believe you can get us back to Earth but there's no point if we remain bound to our demon masters, right? They would just come and get us as soon as darkness fell.' Had Sean discovered something? Was I wrong to keep him at arm's length and distrust him? 'I have been with Nathaniel for a long time; he trusts me, as much as any demon trusts their familiar,' he corrected himself when Meilin pulled a face. 'I asked him whether it had ever been done. Of course, I asked him in such a way as to allay any suspicion ...'

'Sean just get to the point,' I begged. 'What did you find out?'

'It can't be done.' Sean made the statement and let it hang for a few seconds as I thought about asking him why he had started speaking in the first place. Then, he added, 'It can be transferred though.'

'Yes, we know that already. One demon can voluntarily give up the binding and pass it to another demon.' I didn't snap in my frustration, but I got close to it.

'No, no,' Sean stopped me. 'I mean it can be forcibly transferred.'

Meilin and I both stared at him. Meilin shook her head. 'I don't follow, what are you saying?'

'The practice was outlawed by their supreme being long before the death curse. I think it was so far back that no one alive now can remember it, that's how long ago they banned it, but Nathaniel even told me how to do it.'

This was a major revelation!

My eyes were bugging out of my head. 'Sean, do you not think that maybe you should have led with that little pearl of information when you first showed up?' I wanted to knock some sense into his head with a handy rock.

His flicked his eyes to Meilin. 'I would have, but ...'

'But I was cradling my dead friend,' Meilin completed his sentence. 'We know now, Otto, that is good enough.'

'Yes. I'm sorry. Well done, Sean. How do we do it? You said Nathaniel told you how.'

'Yes. I think it amused him to tell me as if he were challenging me to use the information.' The joke would soon be on him, I told myself. 'There is a bit of a snag,' Sean admitted with an embarrassed face.

'What is it?' I asked, almost pleading him to get on with telling us something useful.

'Well, in order to use it to your benefit, you will need to convince a demon to take on the new binding.'

Meilin closed her eyes and bowed her head. 'Of course. It can be transferred but it must go to another demon. That's it then; we're sunk.' Her voice had a despondent edge and her eyes were welling up again, probably thinking that her friend had died for no good reason.

Taking his focus from her to look directly into my eyes, Sean said, 'I think I know of one demon who might help us.'

Antimia, Sean informed us, was a low caste demon with little prospect in the new world that was to come. Sure, she would have a territory of her own; all the demons who survived the war would, that was the deal Beelzebub struck apparently. However, she believed there was a better way for her to advance and she had a personal grudge against Daniel for something he had done to her a long time ago.

'How do you know her?' I asked, curious to hear more. From almost nowhere, Sean presented us with the solution to all our problems and it made me twitchy. So far though, nothing he said was a lie.

Sean seemed to expect the question. 'She is an underling to my master and a thorn in his side. She is quite vocal about her desire to advance and she wants her own familiar.' His words rang true yet again.

It was agreed he would rendezvous with us in two hours. Meilin told him to come to Byron's meeting place as soon as he was able. We would be waiting there for him. He left us to carry out his desperate task which left Meilin and me with time to kill.

'I must tell Byron that Chen is dead.' Another tear escaped her left eye when she said it, the droplet swiped away angrily. 'We have no time to lose now. When my master discovers her death, questions will be asked,' she echoed my thoughts. 'What will you do?'

With a glance to the sky, I considered her question. 'Word must be passed that we are doing this tonight.'

'Byron will help me pass the word.'

I didn't respond for a moment; I was thinking about something else. Actually, I was thinking about two things. The first was to do with the binding and how it could be transferred forcibly by a demon. According to Sean, the demon would need to have the familiar with them and be ready to take on the binding as part of the spell. An incantation tore the binding from one demon and passed it to the next but the demon being robbed would know it had happened – that was part of the deal. It meant all the demons would know and they would come for us. We would need to act swiftly, stealing the bindings and then being freed by the demon just as quickly. The act of giving up a binding was far easier: the demon just had to will it. Could we rely on the demon Sean would bring us to do that? What was in it for her other than some short-lived revenge that would backfire swiftly once word got out. The other thing I was thinking, was that if we were going, then we needed to do as much damage as possible. What that damage might be and how we could inflict it, needed to be discussed.

Suddenly aware that Meilin was waiting for me to speak, I mumbled, 'You should go. I will get to Byron's rock as soon as I can.'

Chapter 29

I hurried back to Daniel's house, hoping to find it empty but rewarded with the opposite; Daniel was hosting several demons. Daniel wasn't very forthcoming about ... well, anything really. I was his slave, so far as he was concerned, so sharing information with me wasn't something he felt any need to do. Despite that, it was clear to me that he was what on Earth they might call a fixer. He provided familiars to demons. I felt sure he wasn't the only one, but he spoke as if he moved in the high-end market. He swapped favours and sold secrets, anything and everything that would help him climb the ladder. For the four thousand years he had been trapped here, Daniel, a demon on the bottom rung, had been steadily working his way upwards.

That was about all I knew, yet it meant the demons now in his house and being waited on by Karen and Rita were there because Daniel was able to do something for them and he in turn would get something from the deal. It was a moneyless society so when he gave someone a familiar it had to be because he was getting something or had already got something.

He was a scumbag to my mind, but he was also handsome, and I could imagine my wife correcting me by saying he was a scoundrel – a much more fitting term for a good-looking criminal.

Spotting Karen and Rita reminded me of my pledge to include them in the escape if I could. I hadn't broached the subject yet but would need to soon or miss the chance. The visiting demons' familiars were gathered in Daniel's kitchen, sitting quietly and behaving. There were four of them, two women and two men, one of whom I recognised as a new familiar kidnapped from his house just a few days ago by me. There was an existing pledge I made to get him home and too little time left to separate him out from the others. I was just going to have to risk it and speak to them all.

I nodded to them all on the way in. Wordlessly, as their eyes tracked me, I walked to the kitchen counter where I found paper and a pencil. They continued to watch me as I wrote a note and held it up. The less we talked the better.

They all read it. Their eyes and facial expression telling me when each of them got to the critical word. Then, content they would follow, I went back outside with them trailing behind me.

Away from the house and in the street that ran outside it, I stopped and turned, waiting for them to all catch up with me. 'Salazar,' I addressed the one man I knew, 'when you arrived here a few days ago, I told you I planned to escape and return to Earth.'

Salazar, an Iranian man with a club foot, the result of a childhood accident, nodded guardedly. 'That's right, you did.' My comment and his reply got mixed reactions from the other three. One woman, an ash blonde who looked Scandinavian to me, laughed; the other's hand shot to her mouth in shock that I would talk about such a taboo subject so brazenly.

The remaining man folded his arms and fixed me with a deliberate stare. 'Escape is impossible,' he stated.

'Which bit do you believe will create the biggest hurdle? Opening a portal or breaking the binding? I will be doing both tonight for everyone who is bright enough to join me.'

He shook his head in disbelief and I knew it was time to do what they all thought impossible. I stole a glance at the house to be sure no one was watching then slid my left hand into the pocket of Franz's jacket. Keeping the glove hidden behind my body, I murmured the incantation and opened a portal back to Bremen. It was where I planned to go later. I had just to work out a few pieces of detail.

FAMILIAR TERRITORY

The four faces to my front all held a different expression but each of them was somewhere in the spectrum of bewildered disbelief. I closed the portal again having held it open for less than two seconds; long enough to prove a point.

As the glove went back into my pocket, I straightened up to my full height. 'I mean what I say, I am leaving here tonight. Word will be passed shortly to give you a time and place to meet. I am going to liaise with Byron soon.'

'Who's Byron?' asked Salazar.

'Beelzebub's familiar. One of them anyway,' said the other man dismissively. 'You are the one who killed Edward Blake?'

'I am. I should have started with introductions. My name is Otto Schneider. I was a licenced detective in Bremen, Germany until a week ago when I invaded this realm to rescue a girl stolen from her parents by Daniel and Edward.'

'You came here deliberately?' the Scandinavian woman asked, shaking her head incredulously. 'Sorry, I'm Freja,' she remembered to introduce herself.

'I didn't know what here was. I only knew some people, including a friend of mine had been taken and I came to get them back.' I chuckled. 'Had I known what I was getting myself into I might have gone to Disneyworld instead.'

'What's Disneyworld?' asked three of the familiars, a mystified look on their faces. Clearly, they had been here for some time then.

I ignored the question, so we could move forward, pointing to the man who wasn't Salazar so he could introduce himself. He was David and from a small fishing town on the Canadian Labrador coast. The other woman's name was Rosita, she was Spanish.

'How will you break the binding that holds me to my master?' David demanded to know, his tone filled with doubt and not a hint of hope. It changed the way the two women looked at me. Until he pinned me down with that question, I could see they were fantasising about the possibility of a life beyond this realm and without a demon master to obey.

'You have every right to ask that question, David, but I am not going to tell you yet – secrecy is key. The less you know, the safer we will be.' The truth I didn't reveal was that I wasn't one hundred percent convinced by the idea of transferring everyone's binding to a demon who would then set them free. I had a plan B, but to be fair; it was nuts. 'I mean to bring havoc to our masters. They believe they have no reason to fear us because they think they can control us. They can render us immobile with a word.' I paused to make eye contact with each familiar. 'But what if they couldn't? Everyone thinks the demons will win a battle against the combined forces of every nation on Earth. Now imagine that battle again with the demons' familiars fighting against them not for them. Are the odds so certain now?'

'Yes,' replied Freja grimly. 'I have seen the army Beelzebub has amassed. He has a million creatures in it, each as dangerous and destructive as the next. He plans to set them loose upon the Earth like a plague. It will sow such chaos and destruction that humanity will lose the war before they even know what is happening.'

The suggestion of a hidden army had been mentioned before.

Piercing her with a determined look, I said, 'Can you meet me at Byron's rock in an hour?'

Chapter 30

The more people I involved the more dangerous the game became. It would only take one foolish human to condemn us all. That was the game, though. As far as I was concerned this had to be all or nothing. The demons held all the cards, so we either went big or we would never go home.

Karen and Rita were on my list, as was Ayla and everyone I had personally brought into this hellish realm. Salazar was going to contact them and spread the word through the network of new familiars and Meilin said she would use Byron to get word out to others. I figured there might be as many as a hundred all told. It was too many, or at least, it felt like too many, but I couldn't change it now.

David, Freja, and the others came back inside where their demon masters were still talking and showing no sign of leaving. There was time yet, but I had more than enough tasks to fill it. I too, could not afford to pussyfoot any longer, so I got on with task number one: renewing my defensive rings. It was a task well-practiced and I could do it swiftly, the whole process took no more than ten minutes, though longer this time because I had to explain what I was doing to the other four familiars. They had never seen anyone manipulate spells the way I did, looking in awe as I created and then called forth one of my defensive barriers. Using one up, once deployed they are spent, I had to redo it, so I performed the spell eleven times which was plenty for my new friends to learn it for themselves.

Just as I cleared the pot and water away, Rita returned to the kitchen.

Pulling her to one side so we would not be overheard, I asked, 'Rita, you have always served Daniel, yes?' She nodded; her eyes cast down as always. 'You can look at me, Rita. I am not your enemy, nor your master. I would be your friend if you would let me.' Slowly her face turned up a little. 'Rita do you like it here?' I asked, my voice as soft and kind as I could make it. Her expression barely changed though I saw a flicker of confusion as if the question made no sense. 'What I mean is. If you had a choice to return to Earth – to home – would you choose to go? Or would you choose to stay?'

'Daniel will never let me leave.'

'But what if he did? What if Daniel died and you could choose to be anywhere. Then what would your choice be? Stay here, or go back to Earth and be free to make your own life?'

Her head dipped again, her eyes choosing the floor over my face. 'Don't make no sense talking about such things,' she mumbled. 'Been here forever already. Can't die. Can't escape. Can't fight back.'

Oh, I was coming back for her tonight. 'Does Karen feel the same as you?' I got a half shrug of noncommittal indifference from her. If I took them home and they really didn't want to be on earth, I could deliver them back. I doubted that would come to pass, and I was determined to take them, nevertheless.

Voices echoing through the house told us the meeting was finally over. Whatever deal Daniel was brokering had either gone well or it had not, but the demons were leaving either way. Their familiars, still waiting patiently and obediently in Daniel's kitchen, all stood up and moved to the front door.

As they passed me, I whispered, 'Get to Byron's rock as soon as you can.'

They were soon gone, and I would need to be too. There was much to do yet. Tiredness would have to wait, perhaps I would sleep in my own bed tonight.

'Otto, attend,' Daniel called for me, certain not only that I was within earshot but that I would come running. This was why we would win tonight; the demons were complacent. They knew they had us. We could not escape and if we ever were to, they would just bring us back. For that reason alone, they allowed the familiars enough rope to hang themselves with, never bothering to watch them too closely.

I responded with, 'Yes, Daniel?' as I moved from the kitchen to find him in the entrance lobby. He wanted me to call him master and doing so would show him how subservient I could be. It was too soon to start doing so willingly, I believed, that great of a swing in attitude was more likely to make his nose twitch.

'You were outside with the other familiars. What did you talk about?' His forehead was creased a little and his eyes pinched. He suspected I was up to no good.

'They were curious about how I defeated Edward Blake. Your former familiar was unpopular to the point that other familiars are choosing to shake my hand when they see me.'

'Is that so?'

'Were you not aware?' I asked, sounding as innocent as I possibly could.

'That he was unpopular? Of course he was. He brought familiars to me. The same things that makes me popular among the demons, is what made him hated among the familiars: they blamed him. I don't think he cared one jot.' Daniel dismissed the line of thought but had another question to ask. 'Have you seen Carenis today?'

Feeling my eyes flare with worry, I coughed so I could cover my face. 'No. Should I have?'

Daniel continued to scrutinise me suspiciously. 'I expected him. He has not arrived, and I do not recall him ever being late before.' He pointed a finger roughly in my direction, pinning me to the spot with it and wagging it meaningfully. 'What are you up to, Otto?'

Faced with a difficult question, I tried to double bluff him. 'I am organising the familiars into a militia to rise up and overthrow the demons.'

Daniel cut me some side eye. 'Do not antagonise me, Otto. It will do you no good. I expect a full complement of familiars tonight, no excuses. I don't care what it takes. You owe me five from yesterday and another six tonight.'

'Eleven in a single night?' I protested and looked unduly put upon.

'It is winter, Otto. The nights are long. I am sure you will manage if you wish to see your wife again this week.'

Oh, I was going to see her all right. I bowed my head. 'Yes, master.'

Five minutes later I was out of the house and running through the woods. The familiars would be gathering now. Bryon and others such as Salazar were spreading the word to those they believed they ought to include. We couldn't take everyone, it was too complex, too likely to fail if we included even more people. However, I was confident we would get most, if not all, of the forty new familiars, plus however many Byron and his friends brought along. I still figured on maybe a hundred. It was a satisfying number.

Even if I wanted to, we would never be able to rescue everyone. There were some who saw their life here as a positive and probably believed the demons would win. I had thought Sean to be one of them but was proving the case to be otherwise. Would he come through for us with the demon?

I guess I was about to find out for as the sun began to dip toward the horizon, though it was still mid-afternoon, I could see figures through the trees ahead of me and there were more than I expected. Far more.

A sea of faces turned my way as I slowed to a jog and then a walk. I could have flown and got here quicker but zipping about in the sky would only draw attention. Byron's rock, high up on the hillside overlooking the vast rolling countryside was obscured this time by the press of people surrounding it. I tried to count them as I drew near but gave up and guessed – it had to be close to five hundred.

Five hundred familiars all looking to me for rescue. A sudden sense of responsibility weighed me down. Even though they were all looking my way, they were still talking to each other, ripples of conversation like a susurration that died away as I stepped between the final trees and into the open.

FAMILIAR TERRITORY

The leading edge of the crowd parted, but not so I could make my way into it, Byron was coming out. Next to him was Sean, the metaphorical frost between them obvious. Before either could speak, a shout rang out from somewhere in the gathering.

'Can you really break the binding?'

No sooner had that question been asked than the next voice shouted, this time a woman at the leading edge of those facing me. 'How will you protect us from being taken again?'

After that, they came as a torrent as familiars who might have been serving their demon master for months, years or centuries all wanted to know what I proposed and how it was that I could pull this off when no one else could. Byron called for them to settle, but I had to raise my arms and wave for them to quieten as I made my way through to the middle. Once I climbed on to the rock and could been seen by everyone, they finally let me speak.

'I can open a portal to take us home,' I announced.

Immediately, it created a fresh batch of questions, the most common of which was how when no one else could.

'The how does not matter. I can open a portal and by doing so, I can take you all back to Earth. Some of you will be keen to get back to families you left behind. Others among you have been here a long time and have neither family nor home to whom they can return. I will take all of you to a safe place. There is an organisation, spread across the globe, they are preparing for the fight that is coming when the death curse fails, and they will give shelter to those that require it and the chance to adjust.'

'I just want to go back to my kids,' shouted a man.

'And you can do so,' I replied. 'I will not control you. No one will, but we must consider what is to come. Humanity will need us to fight for them when the demons descend upon the Earth.' I took a moment to think through what I had already said and what I still needed to tell them before I continued. 'You ask how I am going to break the binding.' I motioned for Sean to join me on the rock. 'Tonight, Sean will aid us to perform a spell outlawed by the demons. It has to be performed by a demon and Sean has found one willing to help us.'

'Who is it?' half a dozen voices asked.

'Antimia,' Sean spoke up for all to hear.

A murmuring passed around the crowd, but no one questioned his belief that she would help us.

'There are a lot of us, and I must stress that I have no guarantee to offer you. We cannot perform a test run to see if this will work because the demon we take a familiar from will know it has happened. It will alert them, and they will come for us. When we do it, we will have to move fast and those who are freed must be ready to defend against attack.'

The suggestion that the demons might come for us before we could escape terrified my audience. Voices rang out for the crowd to question my sanity and their own sanity for listening.

'They will kill us all!' Was a common theme I heard from both men and women.

'How can we trust you?' and, 'How do we know this isn't a trap to test our loyalty?' were two other questions I heard more than once. They deserved an answer, so gave them one.

'Whether you choose to trust me or not is for you to decide. I cannot tell you what to think or what action to take. Earlier today, I killed Carenis the ogre.' My claim was met with disbelief.

'It's true,' shouted Meilin, silencing the doubters. 'He challenged Otto because he killed his shilt escort last night, refusing to collect new familiars for Daniel. Carenis challenged him and he killed Chen when the three of us faced him down. Otto has already gone too far to back out now. This is no trap.'

Thankful that Meilin had spoken for me, I said, 'A better question might be how I can be sure I can trust you? Is there a traitor here tonight? Someone who will run to their master and gain favour by betraying us all? How sure are you the demons will let any of us live when they reclaim the Earth?' I paused again to look out at the faces pressing in close to hear me. 'With or without you, I am going to break my binding and return to the mortal realm tonight. I beg you all to come with me.'

'Why can't we go now?' shouted a woman.

'Yeah, why are we waiting?'

It was Sean who answered, 'Because Antimia is not yet with us.' Then he turned his head to me, speaking more quietly, 'I need to tell them where to go. Antimia wants somewhere she will feel safe while she performs the rituals.'

I nodded, 'Of course. Tell them.'

Sean faced the familiars all looking to us for guidance. 'In two hours gather at the packing plant. There is enough room for us all to fit inside. Antimia will set you all free.'

As soon as the familiars began to disperse, heading home to make sure their masters were tended to and without need for which they might summon them, I grabbed Byron's arm. I whispered a few words to him, waited for him to nod his understanding and let him go. He had a task to do and very little time to get it done. Then I climbed back onto the rock. I needed to find Freja, but I also needed to pick someone I knew from the departing crowd of familiars.

That someone turned out to be Montrose. I whispered a task to him too and then scanned around for Freja, spotting the tall, blonde woman heading down the hill.

'Freja,' I called as I ran through the crowd to catch up. 'Freja.' Hearing her name, she turned to see who it was. 'Freja I need you to show me where the horde is being kept.'

'The horde?'

Chapter 31

'Master they believed every word I said.'

'Of course they did, Sean.' Nathaniel wasn't given to gloating, yet he knew that when Beelzebub put Daniel in chains, he would feel obliged to do so. Then he saw a better option: he would present Daniel to Beelzebub in chains himself. He would get to watch Daniel's face when the truth was revealed. The fantasy brought a smile to his face.

'Should I fetch Antimia, master?' asked Sean. 'The familiars may yet be watching her or me to ensure I am true to my word before they reveal themselves.'

Nathaniel was impressed by his familiar's clear thinking. Sean's testimony would be enough to condemn the familiars, but could he name all those who had betrayed their masters? Better to make sure they were all lured to the rendezvous point where Nathaniel could spring the trap. Beelzebub could decide whether they should live or die so long as he claimed the glory and praise.

'Yes, Sean. Please do that now and make sure you are seen. I want to capture as many familiars as possible. I will collect my lieutenants, they will bear witness to my mastery and spread the word. We will wait inside and out of sight until you give us the signal that they have all arrived. Tonight will be a fine victory and another step closer to my ultimate rule.'

Sean was only too pleased to help Nathaniel achieve his goal. For in so doing, it cemented his own desires. Nathaniel would grant Sean land and power in the new world and though he would continue to pay fealty to his master for the rest of his life, he would be a king among men and have many, many wives. Tonight would indeed be a fine victory.

Chapter 32

Freja looked confused by my request. 'You told me Beelzebub has a million creatures he plans to unleash on the Earth. Where are they?'

Finally understanding my question, she agreed to show me. She said it would be easier than sending me to look by myself. It was far enough away that walking wasn't an option. Even if it had been, time was against us, so we flew, keeping low so we would not be seen, we clipped the tops of the trees all the way there. She insisted we drop to the ground well short of the target and go the rest of the way on foot. The sun was dipping but we would still be visible if we got too close in the air.

'Ironically, it's called the Devil's Punchbowl back on earth. I found that out when I was sent here to work. The demons employ us to keep the creatures inside. It takes a ring of magic to prevent them from escaping and the familiars sent here are well motivated because if they ever let their magic slip the beasts inside break out and kill them.'

I listened intently, but I had questions. 'How would you mount an attack if you were able to?'

She didn't answer, she stuck out a leg to trip me and followed me to the ground, twisting me as I fell so she landed on top of me. I had no idea why she chose to attack me, but I yanked on the nearest ley line as I fuelled up an air spell. I was going to hit her first though it was an impulse reaction.

Until she kissed me, that is.

FAMILIAR TERRITORY

Her lips on mine came as a complete surprise. I hadn't kissed another woman since the day I met Kerstin, but as my brain caught up and reminded me that I shouldn't be enjoying this as much as I was, she broke it off. Taking her lips away from my mouth, she placed a hand over my mouth and a finger to her lips. Her eyes flitted between mine and something ahead of us.

I stayed quiet, acutely aware that her groin was pressed against mine as she straddled me. After another ten seconds, she moved. 'Sorry about that. I spotted two demons going by. I didn't have time to warn you and saying anything would have drawn their attention.'

'So you kissed me?'

'I knew you wouldn't be able to speak with my tongue in your mouth,' she grinned. 'Was it terrible?'

'I'm married.' It was the only reply I could think of.

Ignoring my reply, she nodded with her head, 'The edge of the bowl is just up there a bit. Just listen out for anyone coming, okay. This place is crawling with demons usually.'

It was nearing dark when we emerged on our bellies from the trees to look over the edge. She wasn't being ironic when she called it an edge. The land dropped away steeply, falling to a valley more than a hundred metres below where the ground teemed with beasts. We were too far away to make out what they were. From the edge, it was like looking into a bucket of worms, all writhing and moving over one another to form a giant, indistinguishable mass.

I could only imagine the devastation they might bring to the planet if they were ever unleashed. Barely able to believe my eyes, I tapped Freja's arm. 'We have to go. I still have people I need to collect.'

'Me too,' she replied as we shuffled back from the terrible sight below.

Once we were well away from the edge, I stopped walking. 'I have to make a visit to the mortal realm. I need to set things up.'

'You're going there now?' Freja's voice came out filled with excitement.

'It is necessary.'

'Take me with you.' When I looked at her in surprise, she added, 'Please.'

I had no reason why I shouldn't, so I opened a portal, took her hand, and stepped through.

'When were you last in the mortal realm?' I asked her.

Looking about in wonder, she said, '1973. Edward came for me one night. I still lived with my parents. They must be dead by now. Where are we?'

'Bremen. This is the house of a friend of mine.' Feeling pushed for time, I yanked Freja along with me as I jogged to Heike's front door.

She opened it two seconds after I knocked. 'Otto, are we on already?' She was asking about my intention to return. When I suggested it, I felt I was several days away from being ready. Less than twenty-four hours had passed and here I was.

'We sure are. This is Freja,' I said quickly to get the introduction out of the way. 'I need to know what you have arranged. I'm coming through with about five hundred familiars in an hour or so.'

She blew out a breath through her nose as she accepted the mountain of a task. 'Well, Bliebtreu thought it was the best news he had ever heard. He will move heaven and Earth, pardon the pun. I told him I didn't know how many people I would need but he requisitioned the XX arena. Bring them there, okay?'

'The basketball place?' I pictured it in my head. I hadn't ever been there, but I knew what it looked like from seeing it on television. Bremen had a successful basketball team. A large, enclosed space like that was exactly what we needed to process the familiars. 'Great. I'll see you there as soon as I can. I guess we'd better leave you to get on with setting that up.'

'Oh, yeah. Piece of cake, Otto, you absolute turd. Get going so I can run around in a blind panic for the next few hours.' When I didn't move immediately, she shooed me with a hand. 'Go. Vanish through your portal thing.' Then the door was slammed in our faces.

Good old Heike. She would get the job done alright. Following her advice, I opened another portal.

Chapter 33

I took us back to a point in the woods not far from Daniel's house. I was semi-confident no one would see us and willing to risk it because there was still so much I needed to do.

Freja departed, she had tasks of her own.

First, I checked Daniel was not at home. I expected he would be out; his reason for not travelling to the mortal realm with me was his need to conduct other business. Karen and Rita were not there either, though, which threw a spanner in my plan to take them with me.

Frustrated, I pushed it to one side. If they were not here, then perhaps they were at the warehouse. I moved to my next job. I hadn't seen or heard anything about Ayla since I snuck around to her house the one time. I asked Salazar, but he hadn't seen her either. Determined that I wouldn't leave without her, I went back to Teague's house. It was full dark now, which cloaked my furtive movements, but also meant I could see Teague clearly inside his house because his lights were on. The demon was talking to someone, but from the angle of his head, that someone had to be on the floor. Was it Ayla?

I felt certain it was, and dearly wanted to break down his door so I could fight him and pull her out of there. I even felt my right foot twitch in the direction of his house, but I stopped myself. If I fought him now this was all over. The next two tasks on my list were about to take me past the point of no return anyway.

FAMILIAR TERRITORY

Now doubly frustrated, I went to the house where Montrose was kept as a familiar to Bethusa. I didn't pick him for any particular reason other than because I spotted him first when we left the hill. I approached his master's house from the rear, finding Montrose waiting for me in the dark just inside the house as we planned.

'Ready?' I asked when he opened the door.

'As I'll ever be.'

Chapter 34

Most of the familiars, a small army of them now, were waiting in the trees when I arrived, I knew Daniel would be looking for me by now. There was absolutely no time to waste but there was one thing left to do which had to be conducted stealthily.

Coming out of the woods on our way to the arranged rendezvous point, I spotted shilt guarding the entrance. I knew they would be there which was why I chose to approach with just Tiberius and Gwyneth by my side. Walking toward the shilt, I counted down.

'Three, two, one.'

We each threw a small rock into the air ahead of us and released the spell we were holding. It was a trick I had never thought to use myself until I saw it employed at the duel, however it was one in common practice here. The rocks zipped across the space before the shilt could draw their weapons, each taken off their feet by the impact as the small rocks acted as bullets.

Satisfied they were dead, I motioned for the herd of familiars silently hiding in the trees and pushed open the door. Inside, the large room was almost completely empty. Raymond was there, pleased to see me I think but then startled by the throng of people coming through the doors after me. Karen and Rita were there too, standing off to one side where they waited with clothing for the new familiars I was supposed to be bringing them.

I went to them first. 'Ladies, you are undoubtedly wondering what is happening. In common parlance, this is a jail break. I am about to break the binding between these familiars and their masters and then we are all going back to Earth. I implore you to come with me.'

Karen looked at Rita, but only for a split second. Then she dropped the bundle of clothing she held and grabbed Rita's shoulders. 'Come on, Rita. We have to. This is our chance.'

Behind me as Karen and Rita argued, Meilin asked, 'Where's Sean?'

Her question sent a nervous ripple through the people still filing through behind her and was echoed by those already inside. Worried eyes faced me.

'We don't need him.' Anticipating their next question, I said, 'We don't need Antimia either.' Then I waved them to silence as I proceeded to take off my jacket and open my shirt. 'You are probably wondering why I switched the meeting place and brought you to the warehouse. The answer is simple: Sean was lying.' I never really stopped being suspicious of him even though he always spoke the truth. It wasn't until the very last sentence up on Byron's rock, when I heard him lie. He said Antimia would set them all free and every word of it was a lie that sang out to me. If he lied about that, then none of it was really true. 'Right now, I believe he is at the packing plant with a band of demons led by his master, Nathaniel. He was attempting to lead us into a trap.'

'Then why are we here?' demanded a man as he pushed his way to the front. I recognised him as the familiar I dubbed tattoo when I watched him fight a few nights ago.

His question was followed by dozens of others as panic began to set in. If they returned home quickly, they could pretend they knew nothing about it. They might get away with it, but they needed to move fast.

When I replied, only those closest to me heard because I chose not to shout. Byron was among them, looking at me sternly because he felt I had betrayed his trust. Until I repeated what I said, that is.

'The spell requires demon blood, that is all. I have demon blood in my veins.'

The shocked reaction to my claim was expected and this time waving them to silence did not work. I had to shout instead. 'I already broke the bond between Montrose and his master Bethusa and my own bond to my master, Daniel. Sean and whoever is with him are not expecting you all to arrive for another half an hour, that is why I also brought this gathering forward. The bigger issue will be Bethusa and Daniel, who will by now be looking for Montrose and me. Montrose is already back in the mortal realm and being cared for by people I believe we can trust. I also broke my own master's bond and I am now free.' This was my plan B – the nuts idea I dreamed up because I really wasn't sold on Sean's idea of binding us all to Antimia, a demon I had never met.

'How do we know you didn't murder him and leave his body in the woods?' yelled a man standing barely a metre away.

Knowing this might come, I was ready. With the shilt glove already on my left hand but hidden by the darkness until now, I opened a portal to the hastily prepared shelter in Bremen. 'Tell the others what you see.'

The man and others near him came closer so they could look through the portal to the room beyond. It was the inside of the city's basketball stadium. Heike told me she would be ready and though it was a rough version, there were dozens of people waiting to receive the familiars exactly as I requested. Sitting among them on a fold-out chair was Montrose. He gave a wave.

Struck silent, the man with the dissenting attitude waved back.

'Go first Meilin,' I encouraged as I closed the portal again; I couldn't do both things at the same time. 'Show them what is possible.' Not a sound was made as I beckoned her to step forward. 'I need your hand.' Taking her offered right hand in my left, I cut myself with a small blade liberated from Daniel's kitchen. As my blood flowed, I pressed her right thumb to the wound, moved it to my chest and recited the incantation. 'Mouassa ent unrega.'

A spark of light flashed between her thumb and my chest and when I removed it, her print remained where her thumb had been. It looked just like the demon marks always did; like a brand, until I said the next incantation. 'Ungowa tal may.' The ancient language of the demons was gibberish to me, but the demon mark vanished just as it had for Montrose.

FAMILIAR TERRITORY

'I can feel it,' Meilin gasped. 'I can feel that I am no longer bound.' Word spread backward through the throng of people.

Instantly, I brought the portal back up. 'Go through, Meilin. Show them.' I got a nervous glance from her. She had been here for so many years and left the mortal realm so long ago that to be anywhere else would be a terrible shock. She chose to embrace it, pushing herself to cross between the realms and take Heike's outstretched hand.

When she glanced back at me, I nodded to her and closed the portal again. The moment I did, the spell was broken, and the crowd rushed me in their desperation to be next.

'You need to go in batches!' I shouted to be heard. 'One at a time will take too long.'

Byron pushed to the front, yelling to be heard. 'I think I can link them, Otto.'

'What?' I had to shout to make myself heard as everyone spoke at once, trying to be next and desperate to not miss out.

'There's too many of them. Acadus will have felt Meilin's binding drop. I don't know how long we have, but with two demons already looking for us and now a third, it won't be long before they think to look here.'

What he shouted to me was overheard by enough ears that it started a panic. A surge of people at the back created an irresistible wave of forward movement and suddenly I was being shoved backward by the very people I was trying to help. Shouting didn't work, they were gripped by herd mentality, fear powering them until I shot a jet of blue flame into the air above them.

Startled, they all silenced as if I had pressed the mute button on my television remote.

I exhaled a small sigh of relief but kept my eyes on the faces staring wide-eyed at me when I spoke to Byron. 'Byron, what were you saying?'

'We need to link them together and break the binding for everyone in a single spell.'

I couldn't help but frown. 'You can do that?'

'I think so,' he nodded. 'I have seen such things done. Not with this spell, but it is worth trying. It will take far longer than I predict we have otherwise.'

Driven by a need to get it done, I latched onto the idea. 'Shout instructions, Byron. Everyone do as he says.'

'Otto is the focus,' Byron yelled. 'You are all the conduit. You all need to join hands now! Spread out as much as you can and join hands with the person next to you.'

What followed was a flurry of activity as everyone tried to grab someone else. Much shuffling ensued as the crowd became a snaking line that wrapped around on itself.

'We need to join the two ends to you,' Byron told me. 'This is like casting the same spell but instead of two people touching you and casting it for both of them, you are casting it for everyone captured in the loop.'

Bryon hurried around the room, helping the still-frightened crowd to include everyone and link back to me. It was a mess but he managed to get them there, taking maybe three minutes though it felt like much longer as half the people in the large room begged the others to hurry up and those at the front, hands linked and ready to go, looked behind in frustration to see what was causing the delay.

From somewhere near the back, Byron shouted to be heard. 'I think that's everyone.'

Flicking my eyes to the two nearest me with their hands free and ready, I said, 'Get ready,' then reopened the wound in my hand so they could dab their thumbs in my blood.

The moment they made contact with the skin of my chest, I said the incantation. I guess I expected the same little spark I got when Meilin's binding transferred to me. That was sort of what happened, but it was amplified or perhaps multiplied by the number of people in the room. An explosion of pink light erupted from my chest, blasting me backward and off my feet. I hit the wall half a second later, cracking my skull on a steel upright. Was it better that I was close to the wall and didn't have far to go? I couldn't decide.

Rubbing my head and wincing as I sat up, I saw that the only person still standing was Byron. Everyone else was now lying flat like spent dominoes. Leaning on one elbow, I hooked a finger into my shirt to pull it open. My chest was a sea of red thumb prints, each like a tiny brand, but they overlapped each other and had to be several deep there were so many.

Feeling a little spent, I whispered, 'Ungowa tal may.'

The thumb brands vanished, the red marks becoming nothing as I freed the familiars from their binding.

The first whoop caught me by surprise. It came from a young man. Already sitting up, his head and beaming grin were visible in the middle of the fallen audience. All around him, the other freed familiars were also getting back to their feet, some helping others, many pushing themselves upright but all sharing the joy that it had worked.

The explosion tearing the rear end of the warehouse away to reveal the night sky beyond came as a complete surprise.

Chapter 35

Choking dust filled the air as it swirled in the sudden breeze, and the moonlight outside revealed a lone figure. Daniel glared at me, his hands filled with hellfire and his chest heaving with rage.

'What did you do!' he bellowed.

Drawing my lips back to snarl at him and raising my shield with a whispered word, 'I undid your evil.' Getting thrown backward to the wall as everyone else went the other way meant I was separate from the mass of people by several metres. It made me a target, but he was here for me anyway.

'Incensus,' he growled. But when nothing happened and I murmured the word to activate my first shield, he shouted it again. 'Incensus!'

'Never again, Daniel,' I sneered.

His hellfire orbs came as a salvo, the next one forming no sooner than his hand was empty. They tore into my shield, the first two rending it down to atoms as the power of his weapon overwhelmed my magical defence. I could barely keep up, invoking the next shield in turn just as the previous one dropped. I needed to return fire, but his blasts were knocking me backward, such was their intensity.

He screamed his rage, his empire falling as he watched and all because he chose to force my hand. He didn't hold all the cards and the sudden realisation stung bitterly.

FAMILIAR TERRITORY

As my fifth shield dropped and the sixth popped into place, I drew in ley line energy but seemingly from nowhere, Daniel was assailed by multiple lightning strikes. They tore into him, too many for him to deflect or resist. Mixed in with the arcs of blinding white light were pebbles. Dozens of them striking him and each leaving a wound as he jerked and flailed from the impacts.

Glancing to my left and right, I saw where it was coming from, though I should have been able to guess; the freed familiars were fighting back. Renewed with confidence, the front row were all venting the frustration of years or decades and their combined might was all aimed at just one being.

Yet more ran to join the line now advancing past me as they closed in. Daniel was beaten and though he would recover, he was down on one knee, huge chunks of his body now missing as the familiars continued to tear him apart. Just as I thought they might reduce him to dust and questioning how long it would take for his magic to knit him back together, his broken body was smashed into the ground by a huge boulder. The rock was the size of a minivan and had to weigh ten tons. It broke into two on impact, but the demon was driven a metre into the soil and buried quite utterly beneath it.

In the beat of silence that followed, I half expected someone to start singing, 'Ding dong the witch is dead.'

Then a spontaneous cheer broke out, my attention drawn to Byron, who had dropped the rock with the aid of several other familiars it seemed, their combined efforts doing what one wizard or witch could not.

Yet again, I had to shout to be heard, 'Others will find us!' It was a statement jarring enough to kill the buzz they all felt, and they fell quiet again. It gave me a chance to finish the job and get them all back to the mortal realm where Heike was waiting.

'I'm going to open a portal back to Earth. Get through it and don't look back. Don't use your magic. It will not be safe to do so, the demons will be able to use it to find us, that is how Daniel tracked each of you. The shilt have infiltrated the planet. They see your auras and when you connect to a ley line. An organisation called the Alliance is going to help you. I'll join you shortly,'

Byron said, 'What? You're not coming with us?'

'I am going back for Ayla.'

'Then I am going with you,' he insisted.

Instantly, Freja said, 'Me too.'

Then others joined in, some less willingly but all pledging their effort to help me get one last familiar. I wanted them by my side, together we would feel invincible, but the truth was that they were still mortal, and the demons would be looking for us. Hellfire would kill them, and I doubted the demons would think twice about using it. It had to be me that went and me alone. By myself I would be harder to spot.

A dull thud ended the discussion as all eyes swung to look at the rock pinning Daniel to the ground. He was trying to free himself and it would not be long before he succeeded.

'We have to move. Join hands and get ready!' I was going to open a portal and send them all through. With the help of the Alliance, I would find a way to keep them all safe because I knew the demons would not take this lightly. It would be enough for now to see them safely returned to the mortal realm.

I never got the chance.

Just as I began to murmur the incantation to open the portal, the concrete beneath our feet split in two. Losing my footing just like everyone else, I pitched over just as the ground erupted. I fell sideways at the moment the portal opened and, though it was still connected to me, I lost control of it. As gravity took over and the portal swung around to be beneath the familiars instead of in front of them, they began to fall through it. I held it open until they were gone, most of them vanishing from sight in a tumbling, jumbled mess.

Daniel was coming. Unable to escape the rock, he must have blasted his way underneath the warehouse floor, or perhaps he utilised elemental magic to shift the Earth. The demons acted as if elemental magic were beneath them, but all were capable of it. Either way, I needed to get free and clear right now.

I rolled to give Heike a thumbs up before I closed the portal, but it wasn't Heike and the basketball stadium I could see on the other side; it wasn't anything. There was inky blackness, and my heart chose to thud in my chest as I questioned where I might have sent them all.

Too late to follow them through now, a blast of hellfire pierced the rock and dirt a few metres away to burn a hole in the roof above. I jumped to my feet, let the portal snap shut, and took off through the missing wall.

Staying here to get Ayla made sense, but that wasn't all I had planned. The rest of it was probably nuts, a suicide run if I could be killed, but even with my immortality, I could be caught and that would be a problem. Speed then, that was the key, and I wasted no time in starting the destruction I had planned.

Leaving the warehouse and Daniel behind me, I threw caution to the wind and flew. Manipulating an air spell to propel me above the trees, I stayed close to the upper branches to minimise the chance of being seen and dropped back down into one of the streets I knew the demons inhabited.

I couldn't get them all and the damage I now wrought would have little lasting effect. Igniting the houses with jets of white-hot flame sure was cathartic though. I torched house after house, driving a lance of fire through to explode a window and set fire to the flammable contents within. Walking down the street, the scene behind me looked like a picture of hell; the aftermath of the end of the world with everything burning. The houses set fire to the trees and lit the night sky. I flew again, onwards to more houses, the bigger ones where I knew the higher caste demons lived. Their houses got the same treatment.

Burning yet another house, I jumped when the unmistakable voice of Beelzebub echoed across the sky, impossibly loud like a clap of thunder. 'Generals, to me!'

Chapter 36

In the packing plant, Nathaniel already knew he had misjudged. Several of the demons he brought with him, those with familiars, were all tearing open their clothing to stare down at their chests. Their familiar binding marks were gone, and it could only mean one thing: the familiars had found another demon to perform the ritual. Whoever that demon was, they would spend the rest of their immortal existence in excoriating agony and would be killed the moment the death curse fell, but that didn't matter now. What mattered was that Nathaniel's plan to be recognised as the one who prevented it had failed. The familiars were free. If they could find a way to open a portal, they might be lost forever.

Cutting his eyes to Sean, his familiar said, 'It is Otto Schneider, master. He is responsible. He will have found a way to do this.'

Hatred welled, driving Nathaniel to open a portal. 'Go to his city, Sean. Kill anyone he knows. Kill everyone he loves. Tear his city down if necessary. I will join you later.'

'Yes, master.' Sean stepped through the portal to Bremen, vanishing into the night on the other side.

One of his lieutenants asked, 'What must we do, Nathaniel?'

'We find Daniel,' Nathaniel growled. 'We find him, and we make sure he is blamed for this failing. His familiar orchestrated an escape and must have had help to do so. Some good may come of this yet.'

Running back outside to begin the search for the upstart demon, Nathaniel's eyes, along with those of every demon accompanying him were drawn to the bright glow above the trees. Two kilometres away, the air was on fire as Otto threw more effort into burning down their realm.

Now torn about which direction to go, Nathaniel was unable to go anywhere because Beelzebub appeared. Beside him was Acadus, Martha, and Berthilda, three of the generals. Aksel and Bitrius approached from the other direction.

'Did you think my order to be a suggestion?' enquired the demon ruler.

'My lord we have been betrayed,' Nathaniel blurted, keen to point the finger at Daniel.

Beelzebub raised a hand to silence him. 'Ancient magic has been used. Many of our familiars, including mine, have been unbound. What do you know of this, Nathaniel?'

'Know of it, my lord?' Nathaniel faked surprise. 'How could I know anything of it? In a matter of familiars, I would first look to Daniel.'

'Of course you would, Nathaniel. Your jealousy for his popularity and success are well documented.' Nathaniel tried to argue but was waved to silence again. 'There is no time for discussion, we are under attack. It may be the angels though I do not see what they could gain, so perhaps it is our familiars foolishly attempting to damage us by setting fires. They should have focused on escaping this realm.' Beelzebub looked around to make sure he drove the message home to all his generals. 'Round up the familiars. Find them. Now. All of them. I want them rebound to their original masters by midnight and then I will decimate them myself. One in every ten will be put to death by their masters as a reminder to the others. This will not happen again.'

'You can't.'

All eyes snapped around to see Daniel emerging from the shrubs that lined the packing plant. His clothing was tattered, his hair dishevelled, but all sign of the wounds he sustained was gone.

Nathaniel's top lip curled as he pointed an accusing finger at the lower ranked demon. 'Your familiar did this.'

Calmly, Daniel tilted his head to look at Nathaniel's face. 'How could you possibly know that? Did you have advance knowledge?' Nathaniel's expression froze and Daniel noted that Beelzebub saw it too. Choosing to ignore Nathaniel as if unworthy of his attention, Daniel approached Beelzebub, 'Sire, the familiars are gone. It is true that my familiar is involved. He may even be the instigator.'

'You see. He admits it!' snapped Nathaniel, not realising how weak he sounded.

Daniel continued as if no one had spoken. 'A portal was opened. I believe it was my familiar who controlled it though I do not know how. I only saw it close and the familiars who were there before were gone.'

Beelzebub took a slow breath. 'You believe the freed familiars have been able to return to the mortal realm. Will you be able to recapture them?'

'With time, sire, yes. I saw into the portal, though, they did not travel to one place.'

'The portal was fractured?' asked Martha, surprise in her voice. 'They could be anywhere then.'

Daniel nodded. 'Most likely, it will deposit them back at the place they were taken. They will be spread across the mortal realm. Each will leave a signature we can follow. Each will draw ley line energy and make themselves visible. We could use the shilt to ...'

'No.' Beelzebub made his one word sound final. 'We could do all of those things. It is too much effort for too little reward. The humans would all have died in the first wave of attacks anyway. We all knew that. Only the promise of survival and a share of the land kept them obedient. That and the threat of death. Do you know how many familiars escaped?'

Daniel didn't bother to hide the bad news. He knew Beelzebub would hear it if he tried to put on a positive spin. 'At least five hundred, sire.'

Several of the generals swore, but Beelzebub just nodded. 'It is but a small percentage of the whole and insignificant. Their use in the war would have been as a shield to deter the humans from firing their weapons – a diversion to delay them until it was too late to stop our attack.'

'Sire, do we not need to obtain more?' begged Aksel.

'You treasured them because they were symbols of status to lord over your fellows. Otherwise they served little purpose which is why you employed them so sparingly and how they came to devise and commit an escape without any of you knowing. Except you,' Beelzebub's gaze zeroed onto Nathaniel.

'My lord, I ...'

'Do not lie, Nathaniel. You are not as good at it as you think. I will be interested to hear what you knew of this familiar revolt, but now is not the time. Clearly, someone is setting fires and I wish to know who. A burning house is of no concern but there are other things I do treasure.'

Chapter 37

I had no idea whether the geographical feature really was called the Devil's Punchbowl, but it was certainly fitting when I looked down again on the swirling mass of creatures in it. Fires raged behind me, several kilometres to the south. I hoped they would act as a lure to the demons, drawing them there while I was here. The winter ground was unfortunately too damp for the fires to spread as far and as wide as I might like but they would still spread and there was no fire brigade coming to rescue them.

However, this was the target. If Freja was right, and I had no reason to doubt her, then the demons would set these beasts free upon the Earth to ravage populations. It would create utter havoc as unexplainable beasts, things from nightmares, tore through communities and there were enough here to achieve that aim in every major city on every continent. It would be a bloodbath.

Staring down into a circular valley that stretched five kilometres in one direction and three in the other, what I could see was a heaving mass of animals kept from escaping by magic. I couldn't see any of those who were performing it, but using my second sight, I could see the familiar sight of ley line energy trailing upward through the ground to reach the familiars tapping it. There would be demons here too, several possibly but I didn't need long and would be gone before they could catch me.

Spreading my feet to balance myself, I took a few deep breaths. This was going to be tough. The ability to use elemental magic to control the earth has many uses. I can raise it up to build a wall to keep animals inside like a pen or form a dam to stop water flowing and make a pool. Reaching down into the soil with my senses to feel the atoms it is made from;

I could then draw it to me or push it away. I could heat it or cool it or even lift it and use an air spell to throw it. In the past, I have torn large chunks of it from the ground to bury my enemies beneath, just like I did with Carenis earlier. It can be an effective weapon, but I wasn't strong enough to do that to an area the size of the valley.

Mercifully, I didn't need to. Ignoring the valley floor as it heaved with creatures, I focused my efforts on the steep left-hand side. It rose from the flat base at a sharp angle, continuing up a hundred and fifty metres or more until it hit the horizon. Grunting from the effort, I pushed as much energy into the soil as I could muster, feeling my way inside to grasp more earth than I had ever attempted in my life. Then I closed my eyes and pulled at it, trying to get the entire wall to move as one.

Nothing happened for a few seconds, at least that was what I thought, but the sound of trees smashing into other trees, of rock falling and the startled trumpeting of the ugly beasts below soon reached my ears. I wasted no time being satisfied, gulped in a fresh lungful of air and did the same to the other side. It too obeyed my command and fell to the valley floor, an enormous landslide to cover most of what was not already covered.

It wouldn't kill them all; they were bound to be tough brutes after all, but whatever was in that seething mass of creatures, I felt confident I just killed most of them. Now I could get Ayla and get out of here. There would be other familiars to save, maybe I would come back for them now that I had all the tools I needed, but for tonight, I felt it was time to be satisfied with just one more.

Weary, and in dire need of rest, I summoned ley line energy and manipulated the air to take myself back to Teague's house. I could hope that he wasn't there but resigned myself to one more fight tonight as I pushed off the ground.

The blast of hellfire caught me full in the chest to send me spinning out of control into a tree where several branches did their best to wind me, impale me, and knock me unconscious.

Falling to the ground and unable to right myself, I caught a glimpse of one demon I really didn't want to see: Beelzebub.

The enormous king of the demons was coming my way and he meant to choke the life from me. He didn't see me as much of a threat and hadn't even prepared fresh hellfire as he closed in. Coming to rest on the ground beneath the tree, I fumbled in my pocket for the shilt glove, came up empty and had a brief moment of desperate, wild-eyed panic as I searched for it.

Looking for a single glove beneath the canopy of a tree at night was a hopeless task so it was with great surprise when my left hand alighted upon it. A crazy giggle escaped my lips as my fingers slipped into the glove and I fell backwards through a portal.

I landed with a thump on the cold street outside my house, didn't bother to look about, and opened a new portal to take me back to Teague's house. The devil himself is after me and I stand to defy him. It was an insane thing to do yet here I was about to pick a fight with a demon just so I could uphold a promise I made to return a woman to her children.

For good measure, I spared myself a moment to set fire to the houses across from Teague's. I didn't think any were inhabited by demons, but the raging fires matched the feeling in my soul as I sent a final gout of flame into the trees and hedge at the front of his property.

Then I stood in front of his house and screamed his name. 'Teague!' My chest was heaving as adrenalin and far too much line energy made my heart pound in my chest. 'Teague! Come out and face me. You wanted to teach me a lesson by taking the familiar I wanted to help? Well here I am, ready to learn.'

The front door exploded outwards, flying across the front lawn to embed itself in the soil. Teague then stepped into the dark hole it left, hellfire crackling in both hands and a mad look on his face. I remembered Daniel telling me the demon hadn't been the same since I exploded him, and it made me wonder if perhaps he was no longer entirely whole. Both Zachary and I had absorbed some of his essence; it changed us, enhancing us both in some ways. I was no longer entirely human, though I felt no different. I couldn't deny the ability to recover from terrible injury nor that tonight I performed ancient demon magic to undo the binding holding the familiars here. I was now part demon, I supposed, but what did my gain do to him?

He twitched, a spasmodic jerk of his head as he leered at me and his lips drew back to show me his teeth. But then a flash of light blue shot over my head. It made me jump, the tension and nerves I felt overcoming my need to look and feel in control.

Before I could spin around to see where it had come from, a dozen more followed it, each of them slamming into Teague to blast him back through his door.

This was good and bad at the same time I judged when I ducked and spun to see six demons behind me. Or were they demons? They didn't fire the usual black-red balls of hellfire, three of them still held the glowing light blue orbs in their hands and I realised I had seen them once before. Outside the cathedral in Bremen when Beelzebub last had me cornered.

They were angels.

'Are we cool?' I asked, keeping a spell handy and trying to remember which of my defensive rings hadn't been used yet.

The leader, I assumed, gave a little nod of his head, jerking it to the right. 'Mary, Gabrielle, please check Teague and make sure he cannot retaliate while I speak to this wizard.' Two of his colleagues detached from the cluster and ran to the house. I didn't break eye contact with the one who had spoken but I still saw it when the space just inside Teague's house flashed with more light blue, a response in black-red and then even more blue. A lot of cursing could be heard, all from Teague, but my attention was on the man still holding my gaze.

'We probably don't have much time before Beelzebub arrives,' I warned. 'You do know Beelzebub, I assume?'

'He is my brother,' the angel replied, stepping forward to offer me his hand. 'I am Godfrey.'

'God - frey? Of course you are.' He didn't look anything like his brother that was for sure. Beelzebub looked like a bodybuilder who had been mainlining steroids for years and possibly injecting himself with rhinoceros DNA. Where the leader of the demons was two point five metres tall, his brother, Godfrey, was my height. He was also slightly built with long hair and a beard.

He looked like Jesus I realised.

A sound from the house, drew my attention as Ayla burst from it. 'She was caged in the basement,' the angel Gabrielle reported.

'Otto!' Ayla bounded across the grass to get to me, sweeping me up into a hug.

'We have to go,' I told Godfrey. 'I am here only to rescue her.'

Godfrey nodded. 'I heard reports of the demons' familiars being freed. You are responsible for that and for this destruction?'

'I am.'

Godfrey gave a tiny bow with his head. 'You have caused them harm this night.'

I was aching to escape this place, but even with Ayla equally desperate to leave, I had to ask him a question. 'There is a fight coming, Godfrey. Beelzebub plans to win it. Do you plan to fight for the humans?'

I slipped the shilt glove back on; I wanted to ask questions, but I wasn't going to get caught here. If Beelzebub or anyone else appeared, I would open a portal and vanish.

No sooner did my cursed brain have that thought than two demons ran out from between two burning houses. They were behind Godfrey's group, but got no element of surprise. As the hellfire orbs were launched, I got to watch as two of the angels caught them while two more returned fire. It was five against two, Godfrey electing to calmly watch as the demons were beaten back and down.

Godfrey turned his attention back to me. 'That is not so simple to answer as you think.' I thought it was. They were either going to fight for us to defend humanity from the demons, or they were going to attack us too. 'I intend to defeat the demons, though I believe they will do much of the work for themselves. I am not the champion of humanity though. I champion the planet and I see the devastation your race has brought to it. I will rule over humanity, but to their benefit, not their detriment.' He told me his plan with a kindly, fatherly smile.

'That sounds like enslavement by a different name.'

'Not at all,' he assured me.

'Man will be free to do as he pleases?'

My question was a trap and he knew it, a wry smile on his face when he replied, 'You should go, wizard. My brother approaches. Do your best to prepare for the fight to come. You can be sure that I will win. The demons are too divisive, too fractured, and absorbed by their own self-interest to ever beat me. In the end they will defeat themselves, but humanity cannot be left to manage itself. They will ruin the world and everything in it.'

I had no chance to argue, not that I would have known what to say if I did. He was right about humanity; we were killing the planet. Worse yet, we knew it and took no steps to correct it.

Two hundred yards away at the end of the road, with the flames licking at the treetops, Beelzebub, his generals, and a host of other demons emerged from the smoke.

As I opened a portal and drew Ayla through it, I heard Godfrey's relaxed tone as he addressed the angels with him, 'I think perhaps we ought to withdraw.'

I could have continued to watch; I certainly wanted to. I knew the demons outnumbered the angels, yet they had come to Beelzebub's territory and were able to fight them. Were they more powerful? Was there something in the old adage of good triumphing over evil that came from the dawn of time?

I soon dropped that line of thought as we arrived in the basketball stadium and hands grabbed me. Heike had hold of my arm as she swung into view before me.

'Where have you been, Otto? Where are the others?' The basketball court and the seats beyond should have been filled with hundreds of rescued familiars, but the only ones

I could see were Meilin and Montrose. Meilin left her seat to comfort Ayla, the two recognising the other for what they both were even though they didn't know each other.

Stupidly, I asked, 'They're not here?' The portal looked different when they went through it, Daniel's attack through the floor of the warehouse giving me a problem I hadn't expected. But what did I know about travelling between the realms? I had done it for the first time a day ago.

Feeling sick, I asked myself, 'What have I done?'

Heike grabbed a chair and threw it under my backside as she manoeuvred me back to sit on it.

'I'm fine,' I told her.

She argued, 'You don't look fine. You smell like someone set you on fire. There's dried blood on your clothes and skin and you have that look you get when you haven't bothered to sleep for several days.'

It was tough to argue any of those points. She was right on every count. When she pushed a cardboard cup of coffee into my hand, I took it gratefully and lifted it to my lips as I looked across the room to where medics were giving Ayla the once over. I expected she would check out fine physically; the mental and emotional scars of her time away from home and stuck with Teague might never heal and she would always know what was to come.

'Is this Alliance?' I asked Heike.

She nodded. 'They are not what you thought. Bliebtreu is desperate to recruit you. You and anyone else with powers like yours.'

'To what end?'

The answer came from behind me, Deputy Commissioner Bliebtreu making an appearance. 'To prepare for what is to come, Herr Schneider. There is a war coming, but I am sure you already knew that. The demons and the angels both intend to rule the Earth and all the creatures who live on it.'

'How do you know of them?' I cut to the point.

'The Alliance has been around for a while now. It started outside of Germany, but we were not too far behind. We are a singular entity, divided only by language and geography, but united in our desire to fight that which threatens our way of life. Other unique individuals such as yourself have already joined our ranks in other countries. We will need you if we are to overcome them.'

I had much to say on the subject but across the room, excited jabbering drew our attention.

'There's some kind of battle happening!' shouted a woman with an earpiece in between talking to someone at the other end.

Bliebtreu was on his feet and moving, Heike right on his heels, and as I followed them, so Meilin, Montrose, and Ayla jumped up to follow me.

'Where is it? Bliebtreu demanded to know.

'Just checking, sir,' replied the woman, listening to people speaking in two different locations. 'Voss reported it.'

'Put him on speaker,' Bliebtreu ordered.

The woman flicked a switch on the small device strapped high on her Kevlar vest and Voss's voice echoed into the large room. It sounded tinny but was clear enough for us all to understand.

'The police got over a hundred calls in less than a minute!' His voice was excited but equally under control as he reported. 'Whatever it is, it must be big. I'm on my way there now with Lange and have a tactical detachment two minutes behind me.'

These were supernaturals he was dealing with: two minutes was a lifetime.

'Where?' I shouted as the woman held the switch to send traffic. 'Where is it?'

'Schwachhausen!' he shouted his reply.

My eyes darted to Heike's and we both said, 'Katja,' at the same time.

Chapter 38

'It's right across town,' she all but wailed, knowing if would take an age to get there.

But with my jaw set for a fight, I growled, 'Not the route I'm taking, it isn't.' I was already slipping my fingers into the shilt glove.

Under the lights in the basketball arena, Meilin saw it properly for the first time. 'Is that a ... did you skin a shilt to make that?'

Opening a portal, I waggled my eyebrows. 'Damned right. Neat, huh?'

I intended to just go, but the second she saw the portal materialise, Heike grabbed my arm, making contact with my skin so she would be able to cross as well. That made Bliebtreu move too, pulling his sidearm as he darted forward to join us. I couldn't tell whether he was excited because he knew what the portal was and wanted to try it out or because he knew I would get him to the action swifter than any other method of travel. He sure was in a hurry, though, and he yelled for all his subordinates to follow.

'This ain't the boy scouts!' he shouted. 'Get weapons hot, people!'

I held the portal open long enough for the Alliance personnel, a dozen in total including their boss, to all get through, but had to hold it a moment longer as Meilin, Montrose, and Ayla came too.

'You just escaped the immortal realm,' I cautioned. 'Stay here. I'll be back soon.'

Ayla was having none of it. 'No, Otto. You risked everything to come for me. Let's get this done.'

About ten seconds elapsed between opening the portal and everyone landing safely on the other side, then I stepped through, closed it and opened another one to get back to Katja's house. The moment the shimmering air stilled, I could see her parents' place, a splendid property owned by a complete jerk. Seeing it reminded me the fool was trying to sue me for using magic on him or some shit like that. Twice I had saved his daughter. This would be a third time. A flash of bright light hurt my eyes with its intensity and the staccato report of a gun being fired ignited my need to join the affray.

'Get through all of you. Quickly!' I snapped to get them moving. Bliebtreu and most of his team, aware they were now in a completely different version of Earth were looking about like tourists. I had taken us to Byron's rock, one place I expected there would be no one else and luck hadn't dealt me a bum card for once.

They went through, me holding the portal open and going through last so I wouldn't leave anyone behind. Then I hit the ground running, pulling in fresh ley line energy as I crossed the ground. I couldn't see anyone, but I could hear shouting; cops giving orders that were clearly being ignored and more blinding light coming from the rear of the Weber's house.

Meilin was to my right as I ran and Ayla to my left, both of them readying weapons though I had no idea if Ayla's skills had grown at all since I last saw her attempt to wield the elements. Montrose fell behind, neither as young nor as fit as the rest of us and carrying a little excess he most likely now regretted.

The Alliance team, armed to the teeth with conventional weapons, were just as ready to ditch caution as they kept pace with us, but as I rounded the side of the house, the sight there startled me and I had to wonder how many of us would walk away tonight.

On the lawn ahead, still covered in snow, lay the body of Herr Weber. Red stained the snow all around him; so much of it that I felt sure he must be dead. His wife knelt over him, screaming for Sean to stop as ten metres ahead of her, near a pergola bearing a climbing rose, the wizard threw another spell at Katja.

FAMILIAR TERRITORY

The young girl, not yet sixteen, had tears on her cheeks but facing the powerful Irish wizard, she was holding her own. Stunned by the sight, and unable to take my eyes off her, I watched as she snatched a branch from a tree. She must have manipulated the moisture inside it to cause the break, but to my enormous disbelief, she then fractured it again and again in the space of a second to create thousands of splinters. Sean had to use a great gout of flame to defend himself as the tiny girl sent them his way.

She was attacking him!

'I got your note!' she shouted, never taking her eyes off me. '*I'll be back soon. Don't use magic until I return.*' Then she managed a quick smile and said, 'Oopsy,' even though Sean was trying to impale her with icicles formed of the snow around his feet.

For a moment, I thought it was just Sean, but no sooner did I begin to conjure a spell to take him down, than Nathaniel stepped out of the shadows behind him. He glared in my direction, hellfire orbs already forming in his hands. They glowed like threats as I growled, 'Rudolf,' to bring up my tenth shield. I thought Vixen might still be unspent but in all the excitement, like Dirty Harry, I couldn't remember how many shots I had fired. Ayla and Meilin fell in either side of me keeping close, Montrose was hunkered down a few metres behind us, a garden wall giving him some cover along with the Alliance guys.

It was a Mexican standoff or might have been if everyone didn't start shooting at once.

I think it was one of the Alliance who chose to fire first, the deafening report of an automatic weapon jolting everyone else into action.

Nathaniel leered at me, as he chose to ignore me as a target. He knew I wouldn't die and had a shield to protect those nearest to me. So he killed the two cops as they popped back up again. Both in uniform, they were the first responders, getting here early enough to seal their fate. They were on the other side of the Weber's house, crouching for cover behind the brick structure until the Alliance started firing and gave them cause to believe they might be able to have some effect.

Nathaniel's hellfire caught them both between belt and collar, blasting them back behind the building and out of sight again. I knew they were both dead. With his attention on one side of the house to kill the cops, he exposed himself to the Alliance on the other. Their bullets tore into him, eliciting a whoop of excitement that died when Nathaniel ignored his wounds as if they were a trifling annoyance. He sent more hellfire orbs in reply.

More bullets opened wounds on his body, his face suddenly a bloody mask as the wounds leaked but then healed almost as quickly. He was drawing the fire his way, which left Sean to continue taunting Katja. It had been less than two weeks since I tried to give her very first lesson, explaining what I knew and how I had learned.

As I ripped a lightning strike in Nathaniel's direction, I couldn't help but notice how she stood her ground and produced a blast of snow crystals to combat a lance of flame Sean threw. I could marvel at her advancing skill later. Right now I had to deal with the demon before he killed everyone here.

The bullets were having no effect, so too the stones Meilin and Ayla launched at him, taking them from a gravel path beneath the snow. I noticed it when I first reached out to feel the earth. If the ground is too frozen it becomes too hard to perform an earth spell, the one thing that would at least immobilise the demon. Pushing heat into it would take too long, but before my own brain could make the connection, Montrose shouted the answer we needed.

'Ever seen that movie Terminator when they freeze the guy?'

Meilin had no idea what she was talking about, but I got it straight away. 'Freeze him,' I yelled to all three former familiars as I poured all my effort into dropping the temperature in his body cells. He felt what we were doing and began to resist. I needed to distract him. 'Heike! Get his attention. Shoot his feet!'

I don't know why I chose his feet. Possibly because I figured enough hits would topple him and that would be enough of a problem for him to feel he couldn't ignore it. I don't know if demons have never bothered with defensive weapons such as shields, but I had never seen one employed by them and Nathaniel wasn't using one now when he really needed it. Maybe it was the same complacency that allowed the familiars to organise an escape without the slightest suspicion. Maybe it was born of their immortality, but as

FAMILIAR TERRITORY

Ayla, Meilin, Montrose, and I put all our effort into freezing the water in his body, Heike, Bliebtreu and the Alliance team nailed his feet with a sustained volley of shots.

One of his ankles just blew apart as several bullets struck home, and the demon bellowed his rage as he hopped and then fell. However, his attention never left me and the other familiars. He knew where the real threat came from.

'Get behind me!' My shout came too late for the women to move as the first blast of hellfire mercifully hit my shield. The second orb took it down and when I shouted, 'Vixen,' and nothing happened, I knew I was out of shields, out of luck, and above all out of time.

My call for Meilin and Ayla to use my body as a shield saved them both as the next volley of hellfire struck my chest and flung me backward. I knew it was coming, and though I want to say I was ready for it, no one can take that kind of punishment and shrug it off.

The power Nathaniel could create drove me off me feet so I played skittles with the two women in my shadow but none of us let up on the spell we held, driving yet more cold into his cells. It was working. The next two orbs of hellfire formed in his hands but not as fast as the ones before and when they got there, he had trouble lifting his hands to aim them. Panting from the effort, I had to clamp my teeth together and fight against my desire to stop.

The hellfire flickered and then died. Unlike when I have seen a demon decide not to use it, and it reabsorbs into their skin, Nathaniel's hellfire just winked out and he stopped moving.

I felt like cheering my victory, but when Meilin said, 'We have to keep him like this. I knew she was right. If we let up, he would unfreeze in no time, his demon magic returning him to life.

It turned out she was wrong, or at least, was denied the chance to find out because Heike came out of her position of cover into a two-handed stance, and with a smile, said, 'Freeze, asshole.'

The single bullet she fired hit his forehead. She was barely ten metres away so it was not as great of a shot as one might think, but the Terminator style explosion as he disintegrated into pieces didn't happen. He just fell backwards from the impact and lay still.

With his master out of action, attention could swing to Sean who was still battling a teenage girl and he wasn't winning. The Alliance soldiers darted forward in pairs, covering each other as they advanced across open ground. They were right to be cautious for Sean flicked out his hands to fling a spear of flame that engulfed two of them. His aim was a little off, the clothing catching fire but mostly on their trousers. They had to dive to the snow to put it out as their colleagues returned fire and sought cover. The bullets struck his magically imbued coat, tiny sparks flaring as the rounds failed to find their target

'You picked the wrong side, Otto,' Sean shouted as he sent a pulse of air to fling snow in Katja's face. He followed it up with a salvo of ice spears ripped from a neighbours' roof, but Katja caught them all in a small tornado she shaped and held to her side before releasing it to send the ice back with interest.

Where had she learned this?

Undeterred, Sean added, 'The Demons will win. They were always going to win. Nothing you have done will make any difference to the end result.' I clambered slowly to my feet.

Then I noticed him wince and spotted the drops of blood beside his foot. They stood out on the white snow. Like my shields, his coat could only take so much punishment before the defensive spells in it failed and his had gone.

'The next bullet might kill you, Sean,' I came toward him as I said it. 'I knew you would betray me, Sean, but I forgive you. You can still choose the right side. Drop your spells. End this now and let me help you.'

He laughed out loud, a deep bark that echoed across the snow, but he did drop the next spell, stumbling a little as he swivelled to face me. To his left as I looked across the garden, Katja still held a conjuring in her hands. She was out of breath and still had tears running down her face, but she was braver than expected and certainly more capable.

A beat of silence followed before Sean spoke. 'The great Otto Schneider. Magnanimous in victory. Too blind to see the future. You will not forgive me, Otto. Not when you find out what I have done.' Before I could question him or even react, I saw a surge in line energy.

He was going to attack!

I had that wrong too. The fact that he was surrounded and desperately outnumbered also meant he had an abundance of targets. He didn't go for any of them. I expected him to fight; with Nathaniel frozen he had no one to open a portal for escape, but he could manipulate an air spell to fly and that was what he did, first throwing up a cloud of snowy ice crystals to hide his movement. The Alliance operatives opened fire to put a hail of bullets through the space he occupied, but a moment later when the air cleared, he was gone.

Katja collapsed to her knees, her mother finally tearing herself away from Herr Weber's body to run tearfully to her daughter's side. I thought the danger past but couldn't decide whether to leave mother and daughter for a moment or make sure they were both alright.

'What did he mean?' asked Meilin, straining with the effort of keeping Nathaniel frozen. 'What has he done?'

I blew a tired breath out through my nose and squared my shoulders as I said, 'I'm sure we'll find out soon enough. First we need to send this thing back to where he came from.' Nathaniel lay on the snow, still frozen in the same position, his palms curled as if holding two softballs where the hellfire orbs had vanished.

'No!' shouted Bliebtreu. 'He has to stay here for questioning.'

Was he mad? I pointed to the frozen form. 'This currently is the most dangerous thing on the planet. He cannot be killed and there is very little you can do to ever stop him.'

'He is stopped now,' the leader of Germany's Supernatural Investigation Alliance pointed out.

This wasn't an argument I could be bothered to have. 'You cannot question him like this, and we cannot keep him in this state much longer. It is taking four of us and the same magic that makes him immortal is fighting us the whole time.' While speaking, I had walked across the garden to stand next to the fallen demon.

Nathaniel's eyes flicked across to look up at me and it jolted me into action.

'Quick! We don't have much time. If he breaks out of this state, I won't be able to stop him!' Down on my knees, I was trying to get the shilt glove out of my pocket when Bleibtreu pointed his weapon at me.

It created a flurry of reaction, as Katja came off her knees again, shaking her mother off as she sucked in yet more energy. Meilin, Montrose, and Ayla dropped their part of the spell holding Nathaniel in place as they came to defend me which meant the full strain of keeping the demon frozen fell to me. I swear I felt a vein burst on my forehead.

The Alliance operatives also reacted, poised and looking down the sight of their guns, they advanced on my position.

Bliebtreu growled an order, 'The demon stays here. We will cuff and bind him and transport him to an underground facility where he will not be able to draw on magical energy. He is vital to our efforts.'

'His power doesn't come from ley lines. Demons use source energy.' I saw the ripple of confusion wash over his face. 'This is beyond your comprehension, little man. He goes back.'

Bliebtreu could shoot me if he wanted, I was opening a portal no matter what.

'Last chance.' His voice was almost begging now but he just didn't understand how powerful Nathaniel could be and he was winning the fight against the cold in his body. Meilin and Ayla were standing either side of me with air spells readied, but they looked nervous. Bullets would kill them, and they knew it.

I waved a hand of resignation at Bliebtreu. I intended to bluff him and send Nathaniel back anyway, but he was no longer looking at me. Bliebtreu's eyes had darted up a few degrees to look beyond me and I noticed all the other eyes facing me were now drawn in the same direction.

I found out why when I turned my head.

Katja was floating!

The petite teenage girl was half a metre above the snow and drifting our way. Her hair had spread out from her head, static from all the energy she channelled making it float too, but it was her eyes that got my attention.

They were glowing gold as if filled with ley line energy.

Sensing my chance, I opened a portal with my left hand beneath Nathaniel and touched his face to make the skin to skin contact crossing required.

Katja chose that moment to twitch her hands and all the Alliance operatives including Bliebtreu dropped their guns, some having to dance about to get the shoulder strap off so they could throw them to the snow where they hissed from the heat she had driven into them.

Her voice came out as a husky threat, 'Get your hands off my teacher.'

I gave Nathaniel a shove saying, 'Happy travels,' as he fell through the portal. I closed it instantly and I drew a thankful breath when I finally dropped the spell keeping him frozen.

'Where did you send him?' asked Ayla, her mouth twitching with a smile.

'To the immortal realm,' I replied innocently. 'I sent him home.'

'I saw clouds,' she replied, her forehead creasing.

I couldn't help but grin myself. 'I might have opened the portal a little way above the ground.'

Ayla snorted a laugh.

Around us, the Alliance were rubbing their burned hands in the snow, Katja was touching back down to the ground but Heike was looking worried. She was listening to her radio, the looping wire snaking over one ear to deliver a message that had her looking concerned.

Just as I looked at her face in question, her eyes snapped up to mine. 'Otto! There's been an attack at the hospital. A man matching Sean's description …'

'Kerstin!'

Chapter 39

I began yanking on my glove; I couldn't think beyond my need to get from point A to point B. Heike saw what I was doing and grabbed hold of me before I could open the portal back to the immortal realm. Her reaction spurred Ayla and Meilin to dive toward me just as the portal materialised. I was going with or without them, but it would have been better to go alone. Each time I stepped foot in the immortal realm, I risked getting caught. It was one thing for me to get stuck there, but the demons would kill the others.

As we stepped from the snow and frozen air of Bremen, and into a bright desert environment, I heard three gasps. The point of the portal was that I moved between the realms and I got to choose where I exited each time. Stepping out onto the shifting dunes of the Gobi Desert minimised the likelihood of meeting a demon. Not that I hung around; no sooner were we across than I opened the next portal and landed the four of us inside Kerstin's room.

It was a big mistake.

In my haste to get to her, I hadn't considered what might be waiting and walked the four of us into a lightning strike that put us all down. Coming from bright daylight in China to the dark room robbed our sight and left us exposed. Sean's attack ripped through us as we stepped between the realms, frying my senses as it simultaneously blasted me across the room.

My skull struck the wall and felt like it went halfway through it. Or the wall went halfway through my skull. Either way it hurt like hell and dazed me just when I needed all my senses to work.

'Schneider,' growled a voice from across the room. Even with the concussion dulling my senses, I could hear the Irish twang in his words. He chuckled. 'I'm going to kill you, Schneider. You might think you're immortal, but I reckon I can find a way to disprove that. Let's start with a little fire.'

I heard what he said but couldn't get my limbs back into a functioning state quickly enough to prevent what he did next. The jet of flame that hit my face was like no other pain I'd ever experienced. I think he would have burned right through my skull and out the back if he'd been able to hold the flame on long enough.

I don't know who hit him first, but I heard the report of a gun despite the roar of flame and my own screams and felt the movement of air as elemental spells caught Sean by surprise. Heike shouted something and fired again. I couldn't see what was happening; my eyes were reporting nothing but bright light still, but Sean was fighting the three women. He would be an easy match for Meilin, could kill Ayla with a word, and Heike would be nothing more than the buzzing of flies but the three of them combined were too much in his wounded state.

I could hear their shouts as they fought him and his defiant bellows as he tried to defend himself. Then a sound like rending metal was followed by painfully cold air which bit at my burnt skin.

'He's escaping!' yelled Meilin.

Ayla screamed, 'No! You can't go after him. I'm not strong enough to fight him, Meilin.'

There were hands on me. I wanted to get up, my hands flailing in my blind state as I struggled to find something to grab onto as a point of reference. 'Help me with Otto,' said Heike, identifying herself as the person touching me. 'Otto, you look like crap,' she told me.

'He looks like pizza that fell out of the box and got run over,' gasped Ayla, making sounds like she might vomit.

'I'll be fine,' I whispered. 'How's Kerstin?'

No one said anything.

'How's Kerstin?' I demanded, my voice harder and more forceful this time.

Quietly, Heike said, 'She's gone, Otto.'

I heard the words come out of her mouth, but whatever she said after that was lost to me as I fell into emotional oblivion. I couldn't tell you how long I spent weeping at her bedside, but by the time fresh voices heralded the arrival of hospital security, my eyes were working again and my burns were healing.

The sound of rending metal had been Sean using elemental magic to tear a hole through the wall, the rolled steel inside it getting pulled apart so he could escape. The room was devastated, part of it burned where he laid flame to my head, part of it torn open, and the rest of it gouged and battered from the few seconds of fight between the Irish wizard and the women. The only part of the room untouched was the bed and the beautiful woman lying in it. She looked serene. I could be convinced that she was still alive were it not for the flatline playing across her heart monitor.

Sean hadn't used magic to kill her. It surprised me, but it changed nothing. That he chose a painless method of dispatch sealed his death just as any other method would.

Heike claimed she hit him with a shot when he was trying to kill me but after that he deflected her bullets and battled against the spells Meilin and Ayla threw his way. He would recover, I was certain of that. The demons would heal him once he found his way back to them. I was glad for it because I wanted him to be in good shape when I faced him next. I was going to tear him apart with all the hatred and negative energy he had chosen to create in me.

Security wanted us to stay put until the police arrived. That was until Heike showed them her badge. I wasn't going anywhere, though, and it was hours later when I finally left Kerstin's room and only then because they came to take her body away.

Chapter 40

There was no doubt about my destination this time, no question of where I might go, and I felt Ayla stiffen when we stepped from one realm to the next to arrive outside her house. The New York skyline hung like a backdrop from a movie behind it, lighting the night sky beneath low clouds.

She had been nervous about crossing back to the immortal realm. I couldn't blame her; it was a place that contained nightmares. They would haunt her for the rest of her life. However, she accepted that we had to go there to get here unless she wanted to wait for a commercial flight. She was in too much of a rush to get home to consider waiting. Like me, she knew the demons were coming and it made every day here without them precious. At some point in our lifetimes, the death curse was going to fail, and the demons would unleash hell onto the planet.

That was going to happen, I was certain of it. No one knew when, but the Alliance's determined need to prepare for it could not be argued. Bliebtreu and I had a problem we were unlikely to overcome. He threatened me to get what he wanted and endangered lives. Until he understood how little power he really had, I wouldn't be able to work with him. However, there were other nations I could help.

I was floating loose now; I had no place I needed to be. Sean McGuire had killed my wife. Thinking about it still broke my soul. The emotion of it was still a fresh, raw wound I could barely consider. I would make him pay, I would not be able to rest until I had, but there were other tasks which would demand my time and one of them was returning Ayla to her rightful place.

Ayla pulled away; her home and family beckoned. Turning back to me, her fingertips still touching mine, she said, 'I can't thank you enough, Otto.' There was a tear in her eye.

I wanted to hold her. To hold someone. I was alone in my grief and it hurt. 'You should go,' I told her. 'Be with your family. Tell them what happened, get them ready for what is coming.'

She let my hand go. 'Will I see you again?'

I looked up at the skyline beyond her house. 'Yes, Ayla. The world will need us, I fear. I must try to find the familiars. They are here somewhere. Maybe all in one place, maybe scattered. I don't know yet, but I must find them before Daniel does. Or any of the demons. We struck a blow, but it is a flesh wound and they will recover.'

She leaned forward to kiss my cheek, then ran to her house. I watched until lights started to come on and then walked away.

Epilogue: Beelzebub

He dismissed his generals with a wave of his hand; he wanted to be left alone to think. One of his six generals, Nathaniel had been an obedient servant for several millennia and benefitted greatly from his position. It was becoming obvious that was no longer true but what to do about that remained a decision he was yet to make. Beelzebub was not one for being hurried, so he would ponder it and make a decision when he felt ready.

That Nathaniel was still absent bothered him. He denied any involvement or knowledge of the familiars' plot to gain their freedom, yet he then vanished and had not been seen since. It left Daniel free to speak out against his former superior, though he showed admirable restraint in not doing so. If Daniel suspected Nathaniel's involvement in the embarrassing situation – Beelzebub certainly did – then he chose to keep it to himself.

Assuming Sean McGuire, Nathaniel's familiar hadn't been killed, Beelzebub was going to force him to transfer ownership to Daniel. It was probably the worst and most humiliating punishment Beelzebub could inflict and it would test Nathaniel's loyalty. If Nathaniel was going to challenge for leadership, Beelzebub would rather know sooner and deal with it. There would be no time for distractions and power games when the death curse failed.

Putting thoughts of Nathaniel to one side he summoned Daniel.

When he appeared a few moments later, Beelzebub beckoned him nearer. 'Join me, Daniel. Can I offer you a drink?'

Unsure what the right answer might be, Daniel declined as was his habit, 'No, thank you, sire.'

'I have a task for you, Daniel. You will track down and kill the familiars who escaped this night. They may prove dangerous if left alive to alert humanity and help them prepare. You will be given a new familiar, a powerful one.' He would announce who it was only once he was able to confirm the Irish wizard was still alive. 'Use whatever resources you need, and I also want to you to begin to restock the pool of familiars.'

Daniel couldn't help the surprised look that crossed his face, but he said, 'Yes, sire.'

'You are wondering why when just a few hours ago I said the humans were of limited use. The answer is simply that it will give my army confidence to have a familiar ahead of them as we go into battle. It is time to step up our preparations. The time is nigh, I can feel it.'

'What of Otto Schneider?' Daniel asked.

'He is trivial. If his immortality isn't something temporary, which I believe it might be, then any effort expended on pursuing him would be wasted. He will do his best to aggravate us, but how much damage can one man do?'

'Didn't he destroy a horde this evening, sire?'

Beelzebub smiled down at his subject. 'Yes, Daniel. But it was only one of many.'

The End

Author Note:

Good evening, dear reader,

I guess it might very well not be evening for you, but it certainly is for me. Staying up late while the house sleeps is one of my best ways to get whatever book I am writing finished. This one, while an enormous pleasure, has been quite the graft at the same time. As an example, I sat down to finish editing and tidying with my gym gear on because I was set to throw some weights around in my log cabin tonight. That was five hours ago, the delay caused by my decision to write another chapter. It was the one where the familiars duel.

Familiar Territory is the sixth book in this series and one which I could not quite perceive when I started writing book one. I don't think it is quite like that for most authors when they set out to tell a story. I couldn't say unequivocally either way because I don't know many authors, but I find my stories make up their own minds as I write them. The characters tell me what should happen. As an example of that, I had a big fight scene planned for the end of this book where Beelzebub would come stomping through Bremen. He argued that it was too early for him to make such a big appearance and told me he had some cookies baking so couldn't come out to play even if he wanted to. My wife wonders if my brain might be wired up a little differently to most other people.

The spring arrived this week as temperatures in the southeast of England reached twenty centigrade (68 Fahrenheit). It meant my four-year-old son insisted it was time for his paddling pool to reappear. He has been asking every sunny day since late January, so I didn't bother to argue. I figured it was still too cold, but he defied me to spend two hours in it each day for the last three.

Here in England, we are all in Covid-19 lockdown still. I feel like I have used that as a history marker in about eight books now, though I know it isn't actually that many. The lockdown is about to be extended, though no one knows by how long, and I fear for the sanity of my wife, who, doubly penalised by being enormously pregnant now, cannot do much at home either. I, at least, can have a couple of drinks and pretend I am at the pub.

I'll leave you for now. I have another book to edit and then another one to start, an endless process because my brain keeps coming up with new stuff.

Take care

Steve Higgs

More Books By Steve Higgs

Blue Moon Investigations
Paranormal Nonsense
The Phantom of Barker Mill
Amanda Harper Paranormal Detective
The Klowns of Kent
Dead Pirates of Cawsand
In the Doodoo With Voodoo
The Witches of East Malling
Crop Circles, Cows and Crazy Aliens
Whispers in the Rigging
Bloodlust Blonde – a short story
Paws of the Yeti
Under a Blue Moon – A Paranormal Detective Origin Story
Night Work
Lord Hale's Monster
The Herne Bay Howlers
Undead Incorporated
The Ghoul of Christmas Past
The Sandman
Jailhouse Golem
Shadow in the Mine
Ghost Writer

Felicity Philips Investigates
To Love and to Perish
Tying the Noose
Aisle Kill Him
A Dress to Die For
Wedding Ceremony Woes

Patricia Fisher Cruise Mysteries
The Missing Sapphire of Zangrabar
The Kidnapped Bride
The Director's Cut
The Couple in Cabin 2124
Doctor Death
Murder on the Dancefloor
Mission for the Maharaja
A Sleuth and her Dachshund in Athens
The Maltese Parrot
No Place Like Home

Patricia Fisher Mystery Adventures
What Sam Knew
Solstice Goat
Recipe for Murder
A Banshee and a Bookshop
Diamonds, Dinner Jackets, and Death
Frozen Vengeance
Mug Shot
The Godmother
Murder is an Artform
Wonderful Weddings and Deadly Divorces
Dangerous Creatures

Patricia Fisher: Ship's Detective Series
The Ship's Detective
Fitness Can Kill
Death by Pirates
First Dig Two Graves

Albert Smith Culinary Capers
Pork Pie Pandemonium
Bakewell Tart Bludgeoning
Stilton Slaughter
Bedfordshire Clanger Calamity
Death of a Yorkshire Pudding
Cumberland Sausage Shocker
Arbroath Smokie Slaying
Dundee Cake Dispatch
Lancashire Hotpot Peril
Blackpool Rock Bloodshed
Kent Coast Oyster Obliteration
Eton Mess Massacre
Cornish Pasty Conspiracy

Realm of False Gods
Untethered magic
Unleashed Magic
Early Shift
Damaged but Powerful
Demon Bound
Familiar Territory
The Armour of God
Live and Die by Magic
Terrible Secrets

About the Author

At school, the author was mostly disinterested in every subject except creative writing, for which, at age ten, he won his first award. However, calling it his first award suggests that there have been more, which there have not. Accolades may come but, in the meantime, he is having a ball writing mystery stories and crime thrillers and claims to have more than a hundred books forming an unruly queue in his head as they clamour to get out. He lives in the south-east corner of England with a duo of lazy sausage dogs. Surrounded by rolling hills, brooding castles, and vineyards, he doubts he will ever leave, the beer is just too good.

If you are a social media fan, you should copy the link below into your browser to join my very active Facebook group. You'll find a host of friends waiting there, some of whom have been with me from the very start.

My Facebook group get first notification when I publish anything new, plus cover reveals and free short stories, but more than that, they all interact with each other, sharing inside jokes, and answering question.

f facebook.com/stevehiggsauthor

You can also keep updated with my books via my website:

g https://stevehiggsbooks.com/

Printed in Great Britain
by Amazon